I0831213

Unjustice by Mac Turney 1

UNJUSTICE

Mac Turney

AVAILABLE FROM:

All book retailers by the name of the book - UNJUSTICE

Or, name of the author, Mac Turney

Unjustice,

Bureaucracy,

Inefficiency and

Drugs are the downfall of this country,

But not necessarily in that order!

This book is dedicated to the 98% of the world population who are victims of UNJUSTICE:

To the Jews who suffer the hatred of their persecutors;
To anyone enslaved who suffer at the hands of their masters;
To one group of Muslims who suffer from another group of Muslims;
To the Christians who suffer the hatred of their persecutors;
To the groups in Africa who suffer the persecution of other Africans;
To the spouse who suffers the violence of the other spouse;
To the children who suffer the abuse of their parents;
To the parents who suffer through raising children;
To the animal who suffers the abuse of their master;
To the poor and uneducated who do not receive justice;
To anyone else I may have missed;
And a special dedication to the victims of any "Unjustice" in any country around the world which happens when you get involved with the police or the Court System
And to those in my family who stuck with me.

Also by Mac Turney
Books:
The Working Man and Woman's Way to Wealth
Available everywhere by name or the authors name – Mac Turney

Unjustice

Published by:

Mac Turney

P. O. Box 537

Stanfield, Arizona 85272-0537

First Printing 2009

ISBN

978-0-578-01869-0

Library of Congress Number 2009903722

Table of Contents

Note: After INTRODUCTION and beginning in Chapter 1 all BOLD lettering will be the wording in documents filed with the Court but with personal information as x's or removed.

INTRODUCTION – WHAT IS UNJUSTICE?

Let me say, for the record: I love America, the people and what we as a nation stand for! I do not advocate violence to re-establish our rights! I propose that we the people, through peaceful process, take back our country and re-establish Justice! Other people in other countries may need to take back their rights, too! We probably lost our rights by inadvertence not by plan or scheme.

I am going to make a couple of statements that is going to make a lot of people upset but by the time you finish reading this book you should be convinced that there is no such thing as justice in America or in most of the countries of the world! And, if you still don't believe it then you better hope that you never need the "court system" to win a case even when you are right or innocent!

The first statement that I said I was going to make is this: The justice system in America and throughout the civilized world is not any better than what we see on television or hear about or read in the newspaper about the cruel, unjust or inhumane system of trial and punishment carried out by any of the dictators around the world.

You ask, "how can you say that Mac?"

My answer is, "it is a fact!" However, I do have a disclaimer and that is, the system in America as well as most of the supposedly civilized countries around the world may not and most likely are not as cruel or harsh as the system under those dictators but the end result is the same. You're found guilty even if you are innocent in most cases.

You are given a trial and many times you lose even when you are right. I'm not just talking about criminal trials. I'm also talking about civil trials as well, or any issue that brings you before a judge, magistrate, justice of the peace or whatever they're called in your country.

Now we are getting to the purpose of the book. And that is, how "unjustice" happened in America and in many other countries and what we as citizens of the country need to do about it. I am not just talking about a case where someone received an unjust punishment whether it was money, property or a sentence. I'm talking about something that has happened to all of us. That's right! It's already happened and just like the financial crisis it is going to be very, very, very difficult to fix! But, it can be done.

If you tried to look up the word unjustice in a dictionary you probably didn't find it so you're probably asking me for a definition, since it's my word. Ok, here it is!

UNJUSTICE

I couldn't find the word "unjustice" in several dictionaries that I searched. It doesn't exist! It's not a word! Well it is now! It is a new word and since it is my word I guess I can give the definition for the word so keep reading and you will see what the definition of unjustice is.

The word "just", as far as the (UN) justice system goes, means something done that was morally correct, or perhaps, the legally correct way to do it; it was a just verdict! Or the fine you had to pay was just, fair or ok. It wasn't unjust!

Unjust means that something is unjust or not just;

Injustice means that an injustice was done to perhaps as few

as one individual;

Injustices are a bigger word and may mean that several were people may have been deprived of justice.

"Unjustice", on the other hand, means: "justice" has been eliminated by; perhaps a plan or scheme, conspiracy or corruption and that justice itself is actually controlled by a select few and given to a select few by those who have control of justice.

Definition:

the planned or inadvertent act of allowing the people to be without justice; being without justice by plan or scheme; the act of implementing a scheme to control justice; conspiracy to eliminate justice; to control justice; to control who has the authority to administer justice; to control who gets justice; the opposite of justice by plan, scheme, conspiracy, corruption or inadvertence.

www.theunjusticesystem.com

Now for the second statement: One that is really going to make some people mad. In fact they could get so mad that they want to shoot me or imprison me for a phony charge of any kind. But, I have to say it:

If you do not have a lot of money, don't hire a lawyer for anything! There, I said it.

Lawyers do not represent you in any court action!

They only represent the amount of money you have to pay them!

By the time you are finished with this book you will know the truth and the facts about Attorneys, the Law and the Rules of Court.

Chapter 1

"In my many years I have come to a conclusion that one useless man is a shame, two is a law firm, and three or more is a congress. .... John Adams"

As I write this book I am also involved in a civil lawsuit where I am the defendant and I'm not a lawyer or college graduate for that matter.

I fired my attorney several months ago because of inefficiency and I am preceding on my own, in Pro Per they call it, and I have been deeply involved in this matter for almost a year and, quite often, I wake up thinking about it during the night.

Effort to prove you are right is an exhausting job and takes a lot of time when you are fighting to prove the other party, the plaintiff in this case, defrauded and extorted you and their claim is unjust.

The effort and time spent takes a toll on your body, mind and your family relationship. My wife is under a lot of stress, I am under stress and disagreements are the norm not the exception. And, it takes up a lot of your time, it costs a lot of money for printer ink, paper, fuel to travel back and forth to the courthouse to file documents and appear when ordered by the court, and more.

It was a long weekend with presidents day coming up on Monday, February 16, 2009 and I had to file a Motion by Tuesday as I was loosing the case so I, as I had had to do several times over the past 9 months, put a lot of time into the case. I was thankful that it was a three day weekend; believe me. I had a lot of work to do.

I worked on this Motion over 40 hours in three days and I am 65 years old. I've been sitting and typing and researching and searching boxes for evidence to file with a Motion for New Trial and the effort had worn me out. My bones hurt, my butt hurts, my muscles hurt, my legs and arms hurt and even my brain hurts!

I wanted to be standing at the Court Clerk window when they opened at 9AM on Tuesday but I just couldn't get it all done in time so on Monday night I worked until around 1:00 AM and I went to bed. I decided that I could finish it in the morning and file it a couple hours after the Court Clerk opened their windows.

I woke up at 4:11 AM and the word "unjustice" was on my mind and the thoughts about using that word as a title for a book about the court system and many thoughts about how the court system is so messed up and impossible for the average person to understand, comply with the law, rules of court, or, to even have the time to defend yourself on any action brought against you if you have to work and thoughts about this book and what it should say and that I should inform the world about what is going on with the courts were all racing through my mind. And, the word "un-just-ice", unjustice! There's no such word!

Needless to say I got up and checked the dictionary, then two or three others on the book shelves and the word "unjustice" wasn't there.

I went back to bed and slept until around 6:00 AM and I woke up again, so I got up, made some coffee and went back to work on the Motion that I needed to file and I wrote myself a note about this book.

Chapter 2

Solomon, one of the wisest men who ever walked the earth, if not the wisest, in Ecclesiastes 3:16 says that in the place of judgment, places of justice, the courts - - "there is wickedness".

I believe the word, "unjustice" and the definition of "unjustice" and the thoughts about this book came from the Spirit within me, from God, and deep within me I realized that there are a lot of people all over the world who are being deprived of justice.

I realized that I had to go through what I have been through to make me write this book. It couldn't have been any other way; if I had lived without the challenges that I went through in my life, the book would never have been written so I thank God for all the bad things I have had to go through and for the courage to challenge "unjustice".

You can help! Together we can eliminate the word "unjustice" from our dictionaries and eliminate it from the justice system.

Hey, perhaps that is why it isn't there now. Someone didn't want us to know that thc word "unjustice" existed!

I'm going to write about "unjustice" in history for just a minute and I am going to get the information from the oldest recorded history that I can find which is, I believe, the scriptures.

If you don't want to read about biblical history because you are an atheist or some other reason then skip this chapter and start with the next chapter but keep in mind God wanted you to have this information for a reason and I believe he wants you to become aware of just how bad the justice system has become.

What you read may possibly change your life, or the life of someone you love for the better, or it can change the way your country does things in the courts and save innocent people from unjust suits and convictions, even death, because of "unjustice".

The only thing courts look at is the Rules of Court and the law and they are so complicated that even the lawyers don't understand them but the judges can use them for control and power!

If someone doesn't file a paper on time or if it was improperly filed or untimely filed or maybe not filed at all by you or your attorney – you're guilty and off you go to prison or you lose your house or car or money or whatever the lawsuit was about in the first place.

And, it's been that way for a long, long time!

I'm certain there are many verses in the scriptures that warn all of us about the corruption and wickedness of the courts and judges but this one stands out in my mind:

Solomon, one of the wisest men who ever walked the earth, if not the wisest, in Ecclesiastes 3:16 says that in the place of judgment, places of justice, the courts - - "there is wickedness". That statement, that warning, is as true today as it was back then.

Why are the courts burdened with cases? Why are they always asking for more money for courthouses, expenses, more judges, jails and prisons, enforcement officers and more? Because of "unjustice"!

"Unjustice" has inadvertently or intentionally been allowed to totally corrupt the system and give those in control power.

President John F. Kennedy said, "Ask not what your country

can do for you, and ask what you can do for your country”. I am attempting to do that, with Gods guidance, in writing this book.

The “fixing” of our laws and courts could have ramifications far greater for the good of our country than the “fixing” of the economy. I’m not discounting the need, for the good for our country, to correct the problems in our economy but I do want to point out that the 455 incompetent elected or appointed authorities had a lot to do with the bad economy, and the citizens of the country allowed it to happen out of inattention and neglect or inadvertence.

We need to be more attentive, we need common people who are paid with taxes (after all everyone else gets paid with our taxes) as watchdogs to cover our back against the corruption and unjustice taking control of our government, courts and our lives.

And, the Pharisees and the Sadducees who judged in the days of Jesus were corrupt and firm in their traditions, the law, rigid, covetous and cruel persecutors and persecuted Jesus and sentenced him to death.

It wasn’t the people who sentenced Jesus to death! It was the judges!

It is the same thing today. Did you declare the war in Iraq or Vietnam? No! It was the people empowered to make decisions. But, who suffers the consequences of their actions? We do!

When the government starts a war or some action against another country the government puts out propaganda telling us how bad they are and their government puts out propaganda telling their citizens how bad the Americans are, or whichever country where you may be a citizen. And, guess what, their citizens hate you and me and threaten, harass, talk bad about us or kill us!

So, it wasn't the Jewish people – it was the judges of the Jewish people. The same judges who sentenced the Jewish people in their corrupt courts to punishment, prison or to death. And, who was Jesus? He was a Jew!

It's the same in the Courts in this country! Whenever someone is sentenced to death did the Americans do it? It was the Judge and the system! The Law and the Rules of Court!

The court system and judges are cruel and corrupt and only follow the letter of the law and the Rules of Court and they have done that since the beginning of time. The system, the courts, the judges, the prosecutors and the law are not any better today than they were back then or any better today in handing out sentences than they were back then. They are cruel persecutors and only follow the Rules of Court!

The problem with eliminating the constitution and making the Rules of Court more important than justice is: the poor and under educated never or very seldom, receive justice whenever we are confronted with a courtroom situation.

Chapter 3

"A government which robs peter to pay Paul can always depend on the support of Paul. .... George Bernard Shaw"

Any system or government that is left to its own devices without supervision or control is self perpetuating. Whether by scheme, plan or inadvertence – it progressively becomes bigger, stronger and more powerful and eventually becomes the sole power over everything and everyone!

This may seem far fetched but you need to realize that the system or government we're talking about is not a thing – it's a person!

How is it a person? Because at the top of it is a person running it and all of the employees are working for a person who is their boss!

People have many traits: some are greedy some are giving; some are evil; some have morals; some seek fame or fortune and some seek power!

With power, the system or government or a person, can control their own wealth, fame and desires and they can control how much of these that we are allowed to have. Power is their ultimate goal!

That's why there must be rules in place to control that power!

We have power, you and I, but they have placed controls on how much power we are allowed to have and to the letter of the law, how we can use it.

My wife has power over the home and family, pets, whether she works or not and many things in her life.

I have similar power and the kids have certain powers or control over their actions.

The police have power; the judges have power; the prosecutors have power; everyone has power over something but you better not abuse any of the powers they have allowed you to have or you will go to jail!

The problem with power is when it becomes uncontrolled power! And, the fact is, we have allowed “unjustice” to happen and now we have uncontrolled power in the hands of those in power!

The constitution was written for you and me. It was written to control those in power.

However, there was an earlier constitution written that was even better and that earlier constitution was the laws of God and one of those laws was the primary law. “Love your neighbor!”

If we truly loved our neighbor there would never be robbery, lies, rape, disrespect, or, any of the other 50,000 laws in the law books.

Ok, we can’t live by that law so we need laws and we need lawmakers to write those laws but we also need control over the lawmakers or they will seize power.

So, we write a constitution to protect us from those lawmakers. Laws that they are supposed to live by and we need enforcement of those laws. That was all in place at one time.

The justice system and the governments have slowly and methodically usurped the power of the people! And, if they didn’t steal it intentionally then they have inadvertently gotten it along with full power over everything and everyone.

If you believe you have constitutional rights then you are badly informed!

Take just one – “secure in persons and property” – that’s gone!

The power over that right has been given to the lowly street cop that says “I thought I heard a toilet being flushed so I kicked in the door your honor” – it’s legal. Or the cop that says “I thought I smelled alcohol on his breath”, or, “he was acting suspicious so I put him in cuffs and searched him and his truck your honor” – it’s legal.

I have an example of that power. I was told the following by a 22 year old man who lives in the state of Washington: he said, that he was driving home one night from a friends house in a remote area of Washington and that he was doing about five miles an hour over the speed limit and was pulled over.

The officer wanted to search his car and he was being firm and refusing to let the officer search his car.

The officer put him in cuffs and searched him, then put him in the back seat of the patrol car and proceeded to search his car.

The officer didn’t find anything because there wasn’t anything illegal in the car and he came back to the patrol car, opened the back door and told the young man to get out, which he did.

Then the officer reached into his own pocket and pulled out a small baggie of pot and tossed it into the back seat of the patrol car and said, “What’s this?” “It must have fallen out of your pocket!”

The young man said, “I saw you toss it there!” and the officer said, “Yeah, but you better get some respect or the next time it will be yours!” and he let the young man go on home.

How common is this? I don’t have a clue but I will bet it

happens more than one might like to think.

I can assure you that whichever constitutional right you believe that you still have is gone.

We will discuss more about this later but right now let me add that we need control of the power those people have.

Let's face it anyone can get hired as an officer, become a prosecutor, be elected or appointed as a judge and recent history proves anyone can get elected president even if they only have an IQ of 70!

All they have to be is charismatic or a movie star or have someone with an IQ of 170 write their speeches for them or have an earpiece where someone in the back room is telling them what to say or they mumble something that no one understands and then they go on to the next question without giving an answer to the first question.

Chapter 4

"Just because you do not take an interest in politics doesn't mean politics won't take an interest in you! .... Pericles (430 B.C.)"

Who are these people? Who are the people who control justice and have all this power?

Who are the police and enforcement officers?

They are all people just like you and I and they are subject to making a mistake as much as we are and needless to say some of them are totally dishonest, greedy, self centered egotists who believe they can get away with anything but they expect you to obey the letter of the law and if you don't they will arrest you.

Some of them are honest law abiding citizens themselves who obey the law and rightfully, expect you to obey the law. I hope and believe that this group makes up the majority of the enforcement officers but as times get tough in some countries the system will need more enforcement officers and less honest officers may become more common.

Several years ago I had a business where employees with the skill to do the job were difficult to find. With an ad in the newspaper I got several applicants and I interviewed the one with good training but not much job experience. He was an impressionable young man and worked with the local police department on weekends as a volunteer without pay, so I hired him for the full time, 40 hour per week, job.

It wasn't long and his job performance was questionable. I had to use someone else several times a week to correct what he had done wrong and I called him in to discuss the problem. He said that he had been putting in more hours as a volunteer police officer and was tired from working with them during the night but the time required for that volunteer job had been cut because they hired additional full time officers and he would be getting more rest now.

He worked out ok for a while and then became incompetent with his work to the point where it was necessary to use someone to correct what he was doing wrong at least fifty percent of the time. I called him in again and he explained that the volunteer job as an officer was almost every night now.

I asked him if he was getting paid as a volunteer and he said no, he wasn't, but that he likes the job. I asked him, if you don't need money from work then you should just go to work with them as a volunteer full time. He replied, no! I need a paycheck! And I said, well you are going to lose this job if you don't start doing it right and he said they should have new officers in a couple of weeks and his hours will be reduced.

I said maybe you should take a couple weeks off until your hours there are reduced and then I asked him, why do you do this volunteer job anyway?

His reply was, "because I like the power I have over the people"!

He said, Power over the people? That made me mad and I said, "Well, I like the power I have over people who work for me, so you're fired, come back later today for your final paycheck".

The fact is officers are people and there are some power hungry people out there. I'm certain you have met a few yourselves. And, sometimes those power hungry people get hired as officers.

I'm not even going to go into whether O. J. Simpson was guilty or not because I do not know. All any of us have, is an opinion and unless we were standing right beside the man all night and he never got out of our vision and we were holding his hand we wouldn't know for certain one way or the other.

One thing I feel for certain is: don't believe anything you hear and only half of what you see. Think about that one – you may not have seen it as it really was!

The one thing I saw on the news was that there was conflict about an officer planting a glove that was supposed to prove Simpson was guilty or something along those lines. It appears from the verdict, according to the news on television, the jury believed the officer did plant the glove and found Simpson not guilty and, perhaps for other reasons also.

In any case, I am one of those people who believe that one crime does not justify another crime and if that officer did plant the glove then the jury did the right thing by not condoning or endorsing such criminal actions by someone who is supposed to uphold the law.

After all, if the law cannot live by the law then to what purpose does the law serve? That's right, its purpose then becomes to abuse, imprison and control the people.

Perhaps something along the lines of the following story about police officers that occurred when I was 24 years old:

When I was in my 20's I moved to Fairbanks, Alaska and a

recent flood of the city, caused by the Chena River overflowing, was just receding.

The city had a chief of police and four or five officers under him. Of course, in the 60's, Fairbanks still had that pioneer view of life as it had just became a state a few years before and since even police are people, I would see the chief and more often, the officers, in a saloon drinking and carousing as they do in any city or town.

The officers were all around my age and my brother, who is only one year older than I, went to Fairbanks with me. My brother, being a lot more rowdy and social than I am, met two or three of the police officers in the saloons and they would hang out together and even shared a house in Fairbanks for a few months.

Many of the homes and businesses in the Fairbanks area were empty of occupants because of the flood and it was almost winter so the owners moved outside until spring and planned to return and fix up their places when it was warmer. (Outside means: out of Alaska, or, they moved to the lower forty-eight states.)

It turns out that two or three of the police officers were committing burglaries and other criminal acts which my brother found out about while living or associating with them.

One night my brother and I were in a saloon having a few beers and shooting pool and the chief of police walked in, bought a beer at the bar and sat at our table. We were all visiting for a while and my brother told the chief that the police officers were crooks and told him what they were doing.

The chief looked at both of us and asked if we wanted to sign up as police officers and work for the city. I asked what it paid and he said, I believe, 700 a month. We both turned down the offer because we made a little more than that at our present job.

He said, well I guess I'm stuck with what I've got for officers. And he said, I would rather have four or five crooks that I know about and can watch, than end up with five or six hundred uncontrolled criminals and without officers we would have that many or more doing the same thing.

Our conversation changed to other subjects.

I do want to add however, that in my 65 years I have been in several businesses and have met a lot of enforcement officers and the great majority are fair and honest individuals and to the best of my knowledge are upstanding citizens.

Chapter 5

"Giving money and power to government is like giving whiskey and car keys to teenage boys. .... P.J. O'Rourke, Civil Libertarian"

Who are attorneys? Well the fact is they are people too. And, since they are people they get drunk or do drugs or fight or commit crimes. As one person said, "a law license is a license to steal".

Since there are a great number of lawyers in the world and based on my experience there are good ones and there are bad ones. Let's imagine that there is an "unjustice world record book" and that we have a lawyer who holds the title of the worlds' best attorney and in saying that there must also be the worlds' worst attorney, right?

And, since it is established that there is a best and there is a worst attorney, when and if you find yourself involved in a pending court action and you can afford an attorney, you better hope that you find and can afford to hire one of the best, not the worst.

Let me tell you an attorney joke. There were two guys in prison talking and one of them asked the other "what are you in here for?" to which he replied "burglary, what are you in her for?" and the second guy said "second degree murder". The first one asked, "How did that happen?" to which the second one stated, "well, I stole a loaf of bread from the local fast food store, was arrested and they appointed an attorney for me and he got it plea bargained down to second degree murder"!

Many years ago, I will admit, I had a couple beers and drove to the local store in the evening for some milk and cereal and my girl friend was with me. Now remember, this is in the days when John Wayne smoked and drank, well so did I, and so did Dean Martin, Sammy Davis Jr., and almost everyone in the movies and on television, so I didn't think much about doing that.

I was in the coin business and had many thousand dollars worth of coins in the trunk of my car and of course I always carried a pistol in the glove box in case of a robbery, after all, where are the cops when you need one, right?

Well, as circumstance would have it, the city street sweeper came by while I was in the store and the machine he drove used water to keep down the dust from the sweeper.

I came out of the store, got in my car and started toward the driveway. When I got to the street I looked both directions and could see a police car coming toward me on my left but he was several hundred feet away so I accelerated and proceeded onto the street and across the lane with the police car in it. I was going north and he was in the south bound lane. My tires slipped on the wet surface and I was accelerating so when I reached the dry part they squealed.

The police car and I passed each other and he spun around with his lights on and I turned the corner on the street where I was going and pulled over to the curb.

As he was walking toward my car I rolled down my window and he stared at my girl friend for a minute, he and I were about the same age, and he said get out of the car!

I said sure, what did I do? He said, get out of the car! I said, I will but I'm just asking what I did.

He tore my door open, grabbed me and forced me to the back of the car. I said, look, all I asked was what I did. He threw the handcuffs on me and forcibly put me in the back seat of his car.

My girl friend walked back and asked, what's going on? He said he's under arrest! I asked her to get my unopened pack of cigarettes out of the car – you could smoke in jail back then. He followed right behind her to my car and when she opened the glove compartment he grabbed her, threw her down to the sidewalk and handcuffed her.

He reached in and took the pistol out of the glove compartment and called backup. When they arrived they un-cuffed my girl friend and one of them said they were going to take her home in his car and that they were impounding my car.

I told them about the coins in a briefcase in the trunk and told them to keep them safe and I told them that was why I have the pistol, self protection.

They got the briefcase of coins out of the trunk and put them in another police car.

The next morning a judge let me go home and informed me that I was charged with drunk driving, speeding, excessive acceleration, carrying a concealed weapon and refusing an order of a police officer. Wow, I'm looking at 20 years in prison for spinning my tires, by accident and two beers an hour before all this.

I hired an attorney and paid him $3,000.00 up front as he required and told him the entire story.

When we appeared in court for the first hearing he told me, as we were standing at the table in the courtroom and the judge was on the bench, that the best deal he could get me was drunk driving, speeding, carrying a concealed weapon and refusing an order of a police officer. Great, he got excessive acceleration dropped. I saw red!

Right there in the court room I stood up and loudly said to the judge, "this guy is fired" and I told the story to the judge about the coins, the name of my business right there in the city, the pistol for defense against robbery, the wet pavement, the cop grabbing me and pulling me out of the car and I said the officer must have thought that he was Dirty Harry in the Clint Eastwood Movie and reiterated, you're fired, to the lawyer!

His Honor said, "All three of you approach the bench"! We walked up there, the fired attorney, the prosecutor and I. And, the Judge said, "I'm going to dismiss all of these charges except, saying to me, that I will have to agree to plead guilty to excessive acceleration and allow the court to destroy the pistol and that the fine would be $200.00. I promptly agreed but added, "your honor I can get a new pistol for self defense right down the block". I was young and full of it and in those days we had a few more rights.

He said, "That's my judgment". It was done. I went downstairs and paid the fine.

To be honest with you I feel that was justice. I believe we have a right to be prepared to defend ourselves, our family, friends and property from hooligans and robbers and thieves. After all, I wasn't out robbing people; I had a business and employees, paid taxes and I was just being prepared in case of a robbery attempt.

A little while ago we asked a question, "Who are attorneys?" and I would like to add some more to that question.

Attorneys make a living off the many, many conflicts between people and between people and the law. Since that is how they make their living, and since they are people too, they have the same emotions and greed as other people, well, as some people.

And, since that is a fact we must realize that they realize they can make more money if there are a lot of conflicts between people and between people and the law.

Another interesting thing about this is; anytime any two parties go to court for any litigation whatsoever only one wins. That's right, one out of two, and 50% loose! Only the lawyers win, they get paid. Even the lawyer for the looser wins, he or she gets paid.

So, it behooves them to make the laws so difficult and impossible for the people to handle in court by themselves that they have to hire a lawyer. They are in big demand and their fees are outrageous. Some get a million dollars or more for a single case.

As you will see, when I discuss a particular civil action case later, lawyers do not represent you sufficiently to win your case most of the time. I suppose if you are one of the very affluent with lots of money you can get adequate representation to put forth your case and perhaps win.

For all of us who do not have a fortune the lawyer may only challenge perhaps as little as only one of the allegations against you by the other party and they tell you that should get it dismissed.

By doing it this way they only have to spend a small amount of time fighting for you and they can keep the case within your budget, but to do a good job it might take 500 hours of work.

And, they don't want to turn down your $3,000.00 or $5,000.00, which may be all you can afford, and let's face it 90% of their income is from people who can't really afford an attorney in the first place.

The reality is, 50 hours at a rate of $300.00 an hour is still $15,000.00 that it will cost you for an inexpensive attorney to do an inefficient job representing you.

Whereas, 500 hours would cost you $150,000.00 and even in smaller cases involving something that isn't worth $20,000.00 you may actually need to spend hundreds of hours to defend yourself against a crook that is trying to take something that in reality belongs to you.

So, the price for an attorney is so high that you can't afford one and/or the item or items you are fighting for may not be worth the cost of paying a lawyer just to get to keep something that actually belongs to you!

And, the laws and rules for the courts are so complicated that you really need a lawyer to represent you and without one you probably will not win!

How did this happen? "Unjustice!"

We already know why they complicated the court rules and laws and that is because it creates a demand for their service and they can make a lot of money day after day after day. So now we will get to the discussion on how attorneys actually get to write the laws.

Chapter 6

"A government big enough to give you everything you want, is strong enough to take everything you have. .... Thomas Jefferson"

How do Attorneys write the laws? Attorneys become judges!

And, just for the record, attorneys are: the city attorneys, the county attorneys, the prosecuting attorney, the state attorney general, the court appointed defense attorneys, the attorney general of the country, most politician are attorneys and a whole lot more.

They, attorneys, occupy the bench as the judge for almost every court in the country. They are the judges and the Court of Appeal judges; and the State Supreme Court judges and the Federal Court judges and the list goes on and on.

They write the rules of court; they write the laws; they mead out the sentences or judgment on the loosing party; they are the absolute ruler of their domain, the courtroom.

The problem arises when we realize that judges are people too! They have bad days and good days, some are criminal in their actions and some are upright, some do favors for the affluent and well educated or friends and family, some take bribes and some arrest you for offering it. Some can have the attitude of Hitler and others can be as meek as a lamb. They're people, too! And, therefore subject to the same lusts, greed, temptations, prejudice, hate, love and other emotions that all people have.

Many politicians are attorneys and they have good and bad

within their ranks also.

And, that is why the Constitution was written. Not to deprive us of freedom and justice in the courts but to protect us from “people” with the same emotions and temptations that all people have who become the police, courts and the government in any form.

And, they all take an oath of office to defend the Constitution but that oath is worthless. Unjustice makes it worthless.

Attorneys have a great influence on the actions of your city officials, county officials, state and federal officials, senate, congress and the president. Every one of them asks the advice of the appropriate attorney, whether it’s the city attorney or the attorney general of the country. And, most of them have a personal attorney for personal advice as well.

Read the definition of “unjustice” again if you forgotten what it means.

Consider this; you could have money but nothing else; you could have love and live under a bridge; you could have fame and still not find someone to take care of you when you are sick; but, if you have power you can demand and get all of these things.

With power they can do anything, so they think, and as long as they can take advantage of those that give them that power they will do all within their means to insure that that power doesn’t go away!

In any country the real power lies in the population, the people. Even bad rulers have been overthrown by the people. After all, what good would power do them if they eradicated the people?

They wouldn't have anyone to use the power on. They would have to plant their own crops and cook their own meals.

I'm not saying we the people need to overthrow the power – I'm saying we need to petition those in power, legally, with mail, phone calls or whatever peaceful means to get them to have a congressional hearing regarding the laws and we need to insist that they change the rules of court and the laws to make the courts accessible to the 98% of us that can't pay thousands of dollars for a lawyer to defend us in any court action.

Even the smallest of court actions can cost you thousands of dollars for an attorney. We don't have a law degree, we haven't studied law – they don't even offer it as an elective in high school. And, if we can get the laws changed and simplified, we can handle most court actions ourselves.

The problem is "unjustice". No one wants to give up their power.

Chapter 7

"If you think you don't like the system now just wait and see what happens when the system doesn't like you." Unless we fix it!

Do you remember or have you ever heard of Hurricane?

Hurricane was a black fighter that got framed and sentenced to life in prison. He was innocent but he couldn't prove it. After doing many years in prison a young black boy – not boy – just a young boy, a young guy, picked up and read the book on Hurricane and got interested in him and his life and went to the prison to visit Hurricane.

He got the people he lived with interested in Hurricane – they were white people – just a little humor folks. White, black, boy, girl what's the difference? We are all people and we need to get along. Oh, by the way, most of us do.

In any case they all took up the case because they were convinced Hurricane was innocent and eventually he was found not guilty by a federal judge. The problem is; he had spent a great deal of his life in prison.

The problem is, "unjustice"!

It happened to another fighter who was set up in a bar by his opponent and obviously people who didn't like him, with an underage girl who with all her makeup and the way she dressed and the fact that he met her in a bar it appears that he thought she was of age and after a brief affair, was reported by his enemies, was arrested and sentenced to prison.

Another case that I am aware of consisted of charges of incest brought about by the mother-in-law and her daughter, the grandmother of the teenage girls, who coerced them into saying their father had sex with them. The father was getting a divorce and no one liked that, not even the daughters.

Once he was charged and the dates of the supposed incidents were given to him and his lawyer by the prosecutor, he went to work digging through records and files and located receipts from airlines, hotels and restaurants proving he wasn't even in the same city and sometimes not even in the same state as they were on those dates. He was a businessman, traveled a lot and was never home.

He gave all of this to his lawyer and the lawyer told him that the prosecutor will drop the charges once he verifies these receipts and his lawyer gave a copy of the receipts to the prosecutor.

The prosecutor didn't do what the lawyer said he would do. He told the girls to change the dates and at trial there was a surprise – they changed the dates and the father was convicted of some of the charges. The jury was not allowed, by the judges' order, to be made aware of the date changes.

Not only that but the jury pool, they call it, consists of several lists of jurors and one of those lists consists of all government employees and the prosecutor gets to choose the list for any trial.

The jury on the mans case consisted of police officers, crisis center workers, abuse center nurses, a fireman that was in the police academy and a parole officer. See how they select juries below.

However, even the judge at the end of the trial put in the record that there were serious doubts about the man's guilt but he still sentenced him to over seven years in prison anyway.

On appeal the court of appeals said that several things were not done correctly in court but they didn't reverse the judgment.

The man took it to the state supreme court and was waiting for their decision when a young attorney with the prosecutor's office came to him and said, "If you will say that you done anything I can have you out of here tomorrow"!

The man turned the offer down because he was innocent and felt the state Supreme Court would reverse it and find him not guilty.

But, after they reviewed everything they said that there were "serious doubts as to his culpability" but they still didn't reverse the case so he had to spend the rest of the time in prison.

At one point, one of the daughters came forward and told what happened. She said, they were told to change the dates and told what to say when they got to court by the prosecutor.

And, that she wanted to tell the truth before the trial but was threatened by the prosecutor that if she changed her story now that she would go to juvenile hall until she was 18 for lying.

A few years later the prosecutor was caught doing the same thing to another teenage girl. In this case there was a new element; the girl was the daughter of a high level state government politician.

He had enough power to get an investigation started on the prosecutors office and proved what they were doing so the prosecutor was fired and several others who were involved were reprimanded but kept their jobs in the prosecutors office.

And the other man, who wasn't a politician, after thirty years, finally got the money ahead to hire another attorney and investigators to try to clear his name which may occur sometime in the future.

The one daughter went for a hearing and told what happened and they're still trying to locate the other daughter and others involved for further investigation.

The problem, "unjustice"!

I'm certain you've probably watched on television many times in the past ten or twelve years where innocent people who were convicted of crimes 20, 30 or more years ago were getting released from prison because DNA testing proved them innocent. However, keep in mind, there are many, many more cases where DNA wasn't involved and those guys will never see daylight again.

The reason most of these people were convicted was not because someone intentionally framed them and got them convicted, even though that happens, but because of "unjustice" in the court system and the process itself, the rules of court and prior cases that the judge and jury have determined were "the law".

At times it's the criminality of the prosecutor who just wants a conviction for his record or the police who want to clean up the books and eliminate the unsolved cases or perhaps, as in the case of O. J. Simpson, where, I guess by evidence presented, the cop was so sure in his own mind that O. J. was guilty that he planted a bloody glove that he could tie to O. J. and the jury must have believed that he planted a bloody glove. Maybe he was guilty and maybe he wasn't but it is not justified and it is criminal for any officer to do that, if it occurred.

It is an injustice because of unjustice that has given total control and powers to a select few to determine who gets justice and who doesn't. Unjustice has caused the system to become so corrupt that even the minds of court judges, prosecutors, officers of the law and even the minds of the general public believe that it is the right way to do it.

Propaganda on television, news, newspapers and other media has gotten all of us to the point where all it takes is for someone to be arrested and everyone believes she or he's guilty.

The constitution says we are all innocent until proven guilty. Well that is not the way it works. We are guilty until proven innocent and that is almost impossible to do especially when they have the power to change dates, plant evidence, and control who is on the jury.

So how do they select juries?

If you are registered to vote or pay taxes you will get a notice to appear for jury duty at some point.

The courts already have what they call jury pools. There are several lists in this pool and one is professional jurors. Then there is a pool of all governments workers; and, an A pool; a B pool; and, so on.

Here is the problem with being tried by your peers. There is not a chance that is going to happen.

An individual appearing for jury duty gets paid $10.00 or perhaps a little more per day for the obligation to be on jury duty.

If they have to work for a living they lose their paycheck while on jury duty. Most jobs do not pay them for being off work, even for jury duty, so they lose their income for days or weeks. Most working people try to find a way out; they can't afford to lose their paycheck, so being tried by your peers is gone.

On the other hand professional jurors get paid really good money for every day they are on jury duty.

All government employees receive full pay from their government, state, county, city or municipal job for every day they are on jury duty. They are on vacation and getting paid for it.

If you've ever been convicted of a crime, even a minor crime, you will be excluded from jury duty in most states.

Wait a minute, if I've been arrested then my peers would be someone else that's been arrested and if I'm innocent my peers would be someone who has been arrested and was innocent. Get the point!

The whole thing is a farce but they give off the appearance of a fair trial to the world.

Chapter 8

"Democracy must be something more than two wolves and a sheep voting on what to have for dinner. .... James Bovard, Civil Libertarian (1994)"

If you ever get involved with the court system in America you may end up on the loosing end in a civil case even when you were the one who was in the right and end up loosing your car or home or have to pay someone, or found guilty in a Criminal case and you were actually not guilty and have received some sort of punishment, sentence, probation or fine or a combination of any or all of these.

There is a reason why you lost and that reason is unjustice has corrupted the court system in America and probably many other countries around the world. After you read this book you can decide for yourself whether it has control of your court system. It has!

The problem with unjustice is that it doesn't affect the affluent or the well educated nearly as much or as often as it does you and I. We are the un-rich and un-well-educated 98 percent of America or of any country around the world and it has an effect on us a lot more often than not.

Sure, the affluent and the well educated sometimes lose in a court even though they may have been right or not guilty but not as often as you and I.

The reality is; you and I really don't have a chance most of the time. Unjustice has gained the upper hand in our "justice system".

It doesn't matter if you are white, black, brown, yellow, male, female, gay or lesbian or straight, old or young, a US citizen or an immigrant or a tourist in America and in most countries around the world. If you have a legal issue you could be in huge trouble. And, yes, it does apply to wealthy and well educated also, when things go wrong.

We need a court system revolution! Not with violence, of course!

We need a congressional hearing to change the court system. And we need to be the majority of the researchers and committee members and the initiators of rewriting the laws and changing the rules of court so that we all have fair access.

We're not stupid, we just have to work for a living and maybe we didn't go to college, but we have a brain and we know the difference between justice and unjustice!

Even if we are uneducated or have to work every day and even if we don't have hundreds of hours to research the laws and court rules in an attempt to get justice in a court; we need justice and we need to demand a change in the way the court system works in our country.

And, these un-affluent and uneducated law changers should receive the same paycheck every week as the people we currently pay to write the laws.

This is a very serious matter and if you ever get caught up in the court system you will see what this book goes on to prove and it's.....well.....wow! Messed up!!!!!

There are huge law libraries in every state and it's impossible for you to know the proper case that established the law for any particular situation that you may be in.

There is, right there in the law library many, many cases in the law books where you loose in any particular situation and a few where you win – if you can find it and if the judge doesn't rule that that particular case doesn't pertain to your situation, even though it may be almost identical, and he rules that one of the other cases that cause you to lose your case is the appropriate law – so you lose!

Take the case of Hurricane; they violated every law to frame him but the way the laws are written stuck him in prison for many, many years before his case was reversed.

All of these people, even the president and supreme court justices take an oath to defend the constitution but when they violate it, even knowingly, they don't care. There is no punishment or even a ten dollar fine if they violate the oath.

Unjustice is the problem. It has taken hold so deeply that they can swear under oath of office to you and me, the people they swear the oath to, a covenant, a contract, an agreement to protect and defend our constitution and we in our ignorance have let them pass laws that says they don't have to live by whatever they swear to do and there is no consequence when they do anything wrong. They can't be sued and they don't go to jail. They can even pardon each other.

They write or pass laws or presidential proclamations that single out a particular group of people. Hitler did the same thing.

The next law they pass just might be a law that imprisons people for their color, just you blacks, or just you whites, or just gays, well, you get the point. We need to stop it now!

We, the people, need to take back our country and get it back to where we have justice in the court system by demanding that a new system, by the people, be put in place tomorrow! Write, send emails, start petitions going to get it on the ballot for a vote by the people to fix the court system for the people and by the people as it was done when the constitution was first written.

In fact almost every president of the United States of America has passed laws that are totally illegal, against his oath of office, against the Constitution and they are laws that may be used in many cases to totally take away your freedom, put you in camps or prisons, use you for testing of chemicals and dangerous drugs against your will, select a specific group of people that must, under the threat of imprisonment, comply with his law and the list goes on and on.

I cannot possible address all of these illegal presidential laws and I do not need to do that because there are many books already written on the subject of those laws.

The problem we have with the laws passed by the president is that those laws go into effect immediately in most cases and perhaps are even signed into law without any notice or publication or discussed on the news, so the people, most likely, are not even aware that the law exists.

Another thing that concerns me is once he has passed the law, it's the law, and I am not aware of any instance where any court or congress or anyone has ever reversed or made one of those laws illegal or unconstitutional.

Look at the torture of people under the Bush administration and they kept trying to pass laws to make it legal. Come on, do you really want them to be able to torture you? If you allow them to get away with torturing someone, anyone, because they say he or she is guilty, then you are next! If they are really guilty wouldn't they have enough evidence to convict them in court? Yes they would!

And, prisons are slave labor camps, they make you work there. If they need a computer programmer and you happen to be one, you could be on the list to be put in prison to do that job.

The president isn't the only one that can and does write new laws which change or eliminate the Constitution or any one of your constitutional rights!

The United States Supreme Court does it!

Federal District Courts do it!

Every State Supreme Court does it!

In fact the Superior Courts do it too!

And, believe it or not, even the County Justice Courts, the Municipal Courts and other courts may, by their action in court on any case, do it, too.

How do they do that? Well, it's really simply a matter of their opinion!

Whenever a case is brought before them and after all evidence from both sides has been presented they determine who is correct and a verdict is reached. This process may be by judge or by jury. Once there is a verdict they enter a judgment or order which sets out who is to do what or what the punishment or award will be.

This is supposed to be done according to the law which may be written law or it may be case law where a similar case was brought before a higher court and the case now becomes, sort of, the law for other similar cases in lower courts. But the judge doesn't have to obey that law; they actually can violate your rights or the law and force you to appeal their decision. And, they don't get punished for doing this, and you can't sue. Wow! Not only that but when you appeal you may lose no matter what because someone didn't comply with the court rules. Another, wow!

Another very important thing that they have done is write laws that make them immune from prosecution and even immune from lawsuits! That's right; you can't sue them for violating your constitutional rights unless they give you permission to sue them and who is going to do that?

Chapter 9

"No man's life, liberty, or property is safe while the legislature is in session. .... Mark Twain (1866)"

We discussed Rules of Court a little already but I would like to add more about those Rules.

Court Rules are written by lawyers and judges and Courts, I assume originally, to establish some type of orderly process for the progress of cases, or, they may have been written for power.

Over the years the rules kept changing and expanding to the point that there are so many of them that they are impossible to follow unless you are a law school graduate and have a lot of experience in court or unless you are a judge or can afford the best lawyer.

Many lawyers haven't ever been to court and are not efficient in the law or perhaps in the rules of court so they settle the cases outside the courtroom if at all possible.

And, another reason they want to settle the case without a trial is because they realize that only 1 out of 2 lawyers (cases) that go to trial is won by anyone; the opposing side will lose, so, they only have a 50/50 chance of winning and in most all cases will recommend that you settle outside the courtroom.

In effect, the rules take away your constitutional rights because we were all guaranteed equal rights and justice. The constitution has been eliminated by rules.

The rules take away "justice"!

The rules are so bad that in the interest of following the Court Rules the Judges will deny motions or rule against motions because a rule wasn't complied with, making the rule more important than JUSTICE!

Another thing the rules do is they give the judge POWER! With this power he may, if he chooses, be lenient with the rules on behalf of one party and rigid with the rules on the opposing party. And, with this power, the judge is able to pick the side he wants to win.

The judge can get away with prejudice if he wants and he or she does it in the name of the law or the Rules of Court. He may do this because he doesn't like you for any reason: you're white, you're black, you're Catholic, you're Christian or you're Muslim or whatever. This is not justice!

Rules of Court combined with the law as they do it today is another major problem with the court system.

The lawyer looks for a case law that indicates his client should win the case but the opposing lawyer also looks for case law that indicates his client should win the case.

Both lawyers must follow the rules of the court and if one doesn't the judge might overlook it, if he likes you or wants you to win, but the opposing side better not violate the smallest rule or he catches it and they have a problem or lose the case.

The problem with this is the court, the judge, decides which one wins. He will be able to find something in a case somewhere which justifies his decision and one that will allow the judge to deny Justice and deny a fair trial if he wants to, and pick the winner.

And, like I have said before, the judge can violate everything in the constitution and he doesn't get fined or even a reprimand by anyone, even though he or she took an oath of office to defend the Constitution.

The problem, "unjustice"!

Let me give you an example. Please keep in mind; this is just one case before a superior court in Arizona and the only issue was regarding a house on a lot and the legal battle that is "off the chart" as they say, that will keep you on the edge of your seat.

The case is a case where I personally was involved and the documents filed will pretty much explain the entire case and how it progressed from the start.

What I don't want you to miss is the fact that the "plaintiff" tried to steal a house that I owned, one that she never owned, while my wife and I were on vacation but because of a very inefficient attorney and a biased judge this battle over ownership could have turned deadly. My wife and I and the people occupying the house were threatened with death if we didn't give the house to her, the plaintiff. I was the defendant. She filed suit to get ownership of the house. But all of this is part of the legal battle so we will continue just below.

Another thing I will point out now is the Rules of Court which are impossible for 98% of us to follow to the letter and if you don't follow them you have a problem.

Another problem is even if you could follow them they are written by lawyers to insure they have a job and they're so messed up and unorganized and not in an order that most of us would be able to follow.

Another problem is even if you could find the rules of court and get them organized they change them and you must go through changes published for the last forty years or since the individual rule was changed the last time it was changed. Do you see the point I'm making?

Other problems that I might point out, that you will run into if you are ever involved in a court action and they are: inefficient lawyers and time limits placed on filing or having to file within a set time and having the time for you to do all the research, type and file documents and appear in court proceedings and hold down a job.

The reason for using this case is manifold and as you are reading it I will point out interesting points, proof of the disaster we have in the justice system today.

The goofy thing is this should have been a simple case and should have been through the court system fairly quickly but it kept going and going and going.

Problem: "unjustice".

Chapter 10

"The government is like a baby's alimentary canal, with a happy appetite at one end and no responsibility at the other. .... Ronald Reagan"

I am going to tell you about this case and you will not believe that it could happen in this country. It can happen to you, too! So please read on.

Who is the Plaintiff and who is the Defendant?

The plaintiff is the one who files or initiates a lawsuit. Anyone can be a plaintiff. All you have to do is claim someone owes you money or almost anything else that you can think of and start a court action by filing a "Complaint" with the court clerk. You're the plaintiff.

In this case, the plaintiff is a woman I divorced 15 years prior to this occurrence that had drug problems and after the divorce, I felt sorry for her when, within a couple years, she came crying asking me for help. As you will read about it, you will see that I tried to help with her drug problem and allowed her to move into a room in a home I owned and she ended up extorting me and is trying to steal the home.

A Defendant is the person who says, wait a minute, the plaintiff is not telling the truth. A Defendant is the person who is defending themselves against a suit by the plaintiff and if it's you, you will need to hire a lawyer, or, you can fight the suit yourself.

I married a woman, Tami, in 1989 and in a short time divorced her because of drugs and her other addictions. I later felt sorry for her and let her move into a spare room in my home – that was a mistake. She filed suit to get ownership of my home making her the Plaintiff and I am the Defendant and I am defending my ownership of the home as the case unfolds.

Below is a brief outline of the case from the beginning of 2002 until this date.

Keep in mind that these are quick notes I made to myself as reminders so wording may be wrong and timelines may be out of order.

All the shocking, to me, unheard off, off the charts stuff will come later as we discuss the case itself.

I have taken out names and addresses to preserve privacy.

Actually the criminal objective of the plaintiff goes all the way back to when the defendant met the plaintiff in the late 1980's and married her.

2002

I, the defendant, bought a manufactured home complete with all furniture, appliances, paintings, decorations and draperies from Stameys' Home Liquidators on Pinal Avenue in Casa Grande, Arizona and had it delivered and set up on a lot that I owned and I allowed the plaintiff, at her insistence, to move into one of the bedrooms because I was trying to help her get off of drugs and straighten out her life;

2003

I was building a home on another lot I owned and she wanted the new manufactured home but I told her no and that she would need to look for another place to live;

She had moved in her friend, Annette, who had a drug problem, according to her sister and mother and her friend Yvonne, along with her two children, a girl and a boy, without informing me;

Her friends consisted of unscrupulous drug addicts and her boyfriend, her "fu–buddy" as she called him whose name was John or Iceman and people with guns were hanging out at my house and I told them to leave, get off of my property;

January 2004 to December 2008

In January 2004 Annette and/or Tami were beating the girl in the bedroom and I told them to stop and to get out of my house and they rushed out of the bedroom and told me that I was going to jail. I still insisted they leave my house;

Tami and Annette conspired to falsely accuse me and Tami beat me with a rake while trying to kill me. I escaped back into the house until police showed up and they lied and had me arrested, claimed that Tami owned the home, got a restraining order to keep me off of my own property and away from my records, files, computers, home and property;

Tami began extorting me by using the computers and files that she had control of and threatening to destroy them and more and continued until she got me to enter into a rental agreement with her on the house;

Documents filed with the court by Tami show she was arrested, was released, was re-arrested for violating the release provisions, went to prison and was released in 2007;

Tami demanded a truck and $7,000.00 from me and agreed to leave me alone and did for around one year;

Tami began harassing me in early 2008 with phone calls, sending her boyfriend to my house to threaten me and Monica, theft of my identity (see Casa Grande Police Report, officer Robinson and many additional police reports filed with this court);

Monica and I had moved into my newly constructed home and I had sold the house and property Tami wanted by agreement to another family who were moving into the home;

Tami violated her agreement with me and recorded a four year old document that she gained by extortion and had agreed to terminate;

I promptly recorded the notice of violation and termination of the agreement;

Tami called me and was trying again to extort me into giving her the house and even left messages with the Qwest answering service;

Tami attempted to criminally, with a gang of people take possession of the house and in doing so placed the lives of Officers and others in jeopardy, police reports were filed with the court;

Monica and I were in Alaska and by telephone we retained attorney Howard K;

Tami threatened me and Monica and we got an Order of Protection;

Sept. 9, 2008 I am served with an Order from the court that I cannot sell the home

As I filed in my documents to the court when the judge did that he is assuming that I am going to loose the home to the plaintiff before the case is even heard or decided at trial. That is unheard of! He had already decided he was going to give the house to Tami.

But then I found out later there was a reason for him doing that. They had dated in the past when he was a public defender.

Dec. 3, 2008 TRIAL

Tami received a lot of leniency from Judge Olson, but when I terminated the attorney relationship with my attorney I was told by the Judge that I had to follow all the rules of court as if I were an attorney, and I is not. And Tami received advice from Judge Olson. According to the documents she filed, Judge Olson told her to file a Lis Pendens and also according to her documents, she received a letter from Judge Olson. According to Tami, Judge Olson, who was a County Attorney in 2004, wanted to prosecute me in January 2004 but she wouldn't let him.

I was never asked if I objected to Judge Olson presiding over the matter and I would have objected.

I couldn't present any evidence or ask myself or anyone questions, but Tami could!

I did not have any representation, couldn't ask questions and couldn't present any evidence.

The Attorney I hired didn't do anything most of the day except early in the morning he stated that he had a "continuing objection" to lies and items entered into evidence by Tami which were still allowed by Judge Olson.

The trial was never stopped by Judge Olson even though he had to wake up the attorney for me a few times to ask if he objected to an item entered into evidence.

My Attorney couldn't hear so the bailiff gave him a head set that made his hearing even worse so he removed them and claimed he could not hear.

Judge Olson ignored the fact that the home was being used by criminals for criminal activity which was testified to and admitted by Tami and all of her witnesses.

This trial is an embarrassment to the judicial system and if the court were to rule against me it would be a miscarriage of justice.

Dec. 5, 2008 Notice/Order by the Court

Judge Olson stated in the Notice/Order, "subject to ANY superior claim by ANY third party". In fact there are 3 superior claims as filed in the Notice of Superior Claims filed on Dec. 30, 2008 which remains uncontested by Tami.

Dec. 6, 2008

Tami and some of her gang showed up at the home and according to the occupants threatened them apparently by saying they would blow their heads off and the Officers advised them to get an Injunction Against Harassment which they did by evidence presented to the Casa Grande Justice Court at a hearing;

Later in December Tami tried to evict the family in the Maricopa Justice Court and they filed an answer to the Forcible Detainer and the judge transferred the matter to this court, Judge Olson;

Dec. 11, 2008 I filed a Notice of Termination of Attorney and Motion for New Trial

The reasons and evidence submitted remain uncontested…………….and never were challenged

Dec. 17, 2008 Tami filed an Eviction action in local court to evict the family from the house

Dec. 22, 2008 we filed an answer to her Eviction action

Dec. 23, 2008 Trial on the Eviction action

The judge in the local court honored our answer to the eviction action by Tami but referred the eviction case to the Superior Court – directly to the judge she is using to force me to give her the home

Dec. 29, 2008 Notice of Change of Address by Tami – the Plaintiff

Dec. 30, 2009 Notice of Superior Claims filed by me

Superior Claim 1: Citi Mortgage
Superior Claim 2: the family that was buying the house
Superior Claim 3: Me - the Defendant

Citi Mortgage will file suit and foreclose on the property;

If defendant is ordered to give her his home and property the court would be ordering the defendant to violate a contractual relationship with Citi Mortgage;

If the plaintiff is the owner of the property the family will file suit against her for the thousands of dollars they have spent on the property;

The Defendant has already filed a Counterclaim, a counter suit, against the plaintiff;

The plaintiff did not contest the notice of superior claims and all evidence submitted therein was not and is not contested by the plaintiff.

New Evidence proves:

The plaintiff tried to usurp the home and property in January 2004 when she lied to Judge Goodman and said she owned the home and property and got a restraining order;

The plaintiff extorted the defendant into the Agreement in May 2004 as proven by prima facia evidence submitted;

The plaintiff in documents filed with this court stated that Judge Olson is biased against the defendant stemming from the beating of the defendant with a rake in Jan. 2004 when Tami dated Olson;

The plaintiff had possession of all the defendants' property and used that information to steal the defendants' identity for changing the electricity from her name to the defendants name in December 2004;

The plaintiff did thousands of dollars in damage to the home and property which was unrepaired when the home was vacated as proven by evidence submitted;

The plaintiff attacked and beat the defendant with a rake in January 2004 and conspired with Annette to frame the defendant by saying he hit plaintiff;

The plaintiff used the property and home for criminal activity including money laundering and drug running as proven by the testimony and evidence submitted;

The plaintiff drugged the defendant morning and night when they first met as proven by the evidence;

The plaintiff continued the extortion of the defendant in early 2008 as proven by the telephone messages left by the plaintiff and her brother;

The plaintiff is violent as proven by evidence showing AK-47's and other weapons were being fired on the property and with threats toward defendant and Monica by plaintiff that "those guys will kill anyone I tell them to kill";

The plaintiff received $7,000.00 which was admitted in court and not addressed by the court and the plaintiff received a One Ton Dually truck costing $8,500.00 from the defendant for any claims she may have against the property and plaintiff and received $2,655.03 in electrical use that the defendant unknowingly paid as part of his monthly bills which are all owed to the defendant by the plaintiff;

The plaintiff through her friends who moved her items from the home in Dec. 2005 took thousands of dollars in property that belonged to the defendant;

Proof submitted prove that the plaintiff seized, by lying to judge Goodman, all of defendants personal property, business records, computers, home, property and everything the defendants owned and used these to extort the defendant into an agreement by placing many of the items on the back porch, in the rain, destroying some of it;

Proof submitted prove the plaintiff – during the extortion – threatened to sue the defendant for getting hurt on his property and released with a note the threat when the defendant entered into the agreement with the plaintiff;

Proof submitted prove that this court ignored the facts showing the plaintiff violated many of the terms of the agreement and especially the court ignored the fact that the plaintiff and her witnesses were using the home for drug running and money laundering and other criminal activity;

The plaintiffs' criminal mindset was proven with evidence submitted showing many police reports and police involved incidents with the plaintiff where this property is involved including threatening to kill people as proven by the Order of Protection and the Order against Harassment submitted as well as proof submitted shows the criminal intent of the plaintiff as far back as 1989 when she put drugs in the defendants' coffee morning and night; again at the store/café when plaintiff, her family and friends were stealing defendants property and lied to the Sheriffs' Deputy; again in January 2004 when her and Annette conspired to frame the defendant, beat him with a rake, had him arrested and more; again from January 2004 until defendant entered into an agreement with her when she extorted the defendant into the agreement; again by changing the electricity to the name of the defendant in December 2004; again when she took the one ton truck and a check for $7,000.00 and agreed that she was “paid in full” for any claim she has against the defendant; again when she tried to forcefully usurp the home in early 2008 and again when she filed this court matter.

The plaintiff continued to try to extort the defendant when they threatened him on the telephone in mid 2008;

The plaintiff lied in the documents filed with the court as proven and again under oath on the witness stand in the court;

Evidence submitted prove the plaintiff accepted ownership of the one ton truck and that it was being used to tow a vehicle that was used in a homicide in Phoenix;

Evidence proves the plaintiff and her friends who testified that they were involved in drug running and were using the home and property for unlawful criminal activity;

Evidence and testimony by the plaintiff proves that she forged checks using her dead fathers’ signature and lied to the court in the Lis Pendens filed with the court by saying that she made those payments to the defendant;

Evidence and testimony by the plaintiff proves that she tried to manipulate the court system by filing bankruptcy to avoid paying money to the defendant and that she admitted she owed the money to the defendant when she listed him as a debt in her bankruptcy proceeding;

Evidence and testimony by the fiancé of the plaintiff, Fabian, prove that he vacated the property in behalf of the plaintiff with her full authority and was acting in her behalf.

On several different dates calls were made to the court clerks to ascertain information about any filings in this matter but the defendant was told that the file is in the Judges' chambers and they can't tell defendant or get access to the files.

Jan. 13, 2009 defendant filed a Motion for Ruling on New Trial

Jan. 23, 2009 Motion for Ruling on Superior Claims filed by defendant

Jan. 26, 2009 Counterclaim filed by the defendant

Which was for the damages to the home and theft of furnishings.

Jan. 30, 2009 attorney K withdraws from matter due to termination

Feb. 3, 2009 Motion to Amend Payment Record filed by defendant

Asking court to grant proper credit for the $7,000.00 paid to the plaintiff and proper credit for the $8,500.00 one ton dually truck and the $2,655.03 electric bill owed by the plaintiff to the defendant as credit off of all payments made in 2006 and most of 2005 which the court appears to be considering granting to plaintiff;

Feb. 4, 2009 Application for Order and Judgment filed by defendant

Proper Application was filed under the law and rules of court as all three superior claims are uncontested.

Feb. 9, 2009 Notice of Contact Phone Numbers filed by defendant

Contact phone numbers were given to the court for the telephonic hearing scheduled for Friday the 13th of February at 10:00 AM.

Feb. 13, 2009 Status review by the court was previously set as a telephonic review

When I received the Order issued by the court on Dec. 5, 2008 and after reading it I called the assistant to the judge as advised in the order and she said that no one would be present, it is a telephonic (over the telephone) review, she said. I filed a Notice of Contact Phone

Numbers on Feb. 9, 2009, even though all the documents I have filed include a telephone number on the top of the document because I didn't trust the judge or the court.

The telephonic review was scheduled for 10:00 AM on the 13th so I called the court assistant at 9:50 AM to make sure that someone was going to call me. They said it was a court room review! What? I was lied to! I asked if the plaintiff was there and they said yes. The person who answered the phone said let me take your number to the judge so the court can call you. Wow, this is crazy!

The court called shortly after 10:00 AM and the review was started by the judge.

The judge named off everything I had filed one at a time and denied it. I could not believe it. Most of them he didn't state a reason for denying them but on one or two he said premature (meaning it was filed before I was supposed to file it), in other words, it was against the court rules. He didn't sound like he had read any of them, just named the names of the motion or notice or stay or application or whatever, so I tried to argue the case with him and he denied my arguments.

He was going to order me to give her my house and she said something about an eviction of the people in the house so he said he would look for the papers and make a ruling on Feb. 23, 2009. I'm glad she asked about the eviction otherwise he would have ordered me to give her the house on the 13th.

In any case these few extra days gave me time to try to find something else in the law that was legal to file by the court rules.

Feb. 17, 2009 I filed a Motion for New Trial based on Rule 59(a) 4

Feb. 17, 2009 I filed an Application for Order of New Trial on Rule 59(a) 4

Feb. 17, 2009 I filed a Motion for Hearing on merits of Motion for New Trial

I filed these in the order above to comply with the court rules. Out of order, they're dismissed.

I spent over 40 hours of research and typing during the three day weekend, Saturday through Monday to get them ready for filing on Tuesday the 17th. The 23rd comes quick and I wanted to make sure I got them in on the 17th.

Feb. 23, 2009 I filed a Notice of Typing Error by the Court in Status Review regarding the typed record for the review on Feb. 13, 2009

On the 20th I received through the mail a typed document stating what transpired and what was said during the hearing on the 13th. It was wrong. Things prepared by the court did not say what was said correctly. It even said that I had offered her the house for $1,000.00 a month for 40 months and it would be paid for. Wow, what is going on here? I didn't say any such thing! Luckily she turned down the offer according to the document.

I kept calling the court all day and even asked the clerk when I filed the Notice of Typing Error if the judge had made a ruling yet. Finally I got an answer and was told that there was an entry in the file that said the judge was going to pull it for review on March 16, 2009.

I couldn't believe it. I actually got more time to look through everything to see what I missed.

March 9, 2009 I filed an Application for Order and Notice of Additional Fraud and Criminal Activity by the Plaintiff.

She lied to the recorder when she recorded a document at the very beginning.

March 10, 2009 I filed an Application for Order

This one gave the judge one option: dismiss the suit by the plaintiff because of the fraud that I filed yesterday.

March 19, 2009 I called judges assistant. She is typing the order & it is lengthy so do not expect it today and possibly not even tomorrow. I called back on the 20th but no one answered the phone until the last call I made at 4:25 and the guy that answered said for me to call back on Monday.

March 23, 2009 I called and went to the court clerk – nothing has been filed.

March 24, 2009 I called and there has not been anything filed yet.

March 25, 2009 I called and the judges' assistant said the Order went into the mail this morning. I also checked with the clerks' office at 4:00 PM and she said it wasn't in the file yet.

March 26, 2009 I received the court Notice/Order dated 3/24/09

March 27, 2009 I received the Final Order/Judgment

To this date the judge has not dismissed the suit or granted any motion that I have filed or ruled that I am entitled to a new trial!

In fact, the judge has denied everything that I have brought before him!

The information above is my notes and only a brief outline of the case.

Each date/item will be explained in detail later in this book.

Chapter 11

"Unjustice" is not something we should laugh off – we need to fix it!"

I am going to start in January 2004 and progress through this case to it conclusion. The Unjustice still has not been resolved.

As you will read more about later in this book, I had allowed a drug addict that I had divorced in 1994 to live in one of the bedrooms in my home because she asked me to help her get off drugs and, as I had done before, I let her move in.

I felt sorry for her and actually thought maybe she would give up the drug problem and I was just trying to help her get on her own two feet and then she could move and become a contributing member of society somewhere else, away from me and on her own.

During most of 2003 I had been building a home on a lot next door to the manufactured home where I lived, and where she was staying, and almost had it completed by January 2004.

She had the nerve to ask me to let her have the house, where she was staying, when I finished the home next door, even though she didn't work and did not have any income. The house had a mortgage on it with payments that had to be made so I asked her how she could make the payments.

She said that she would get a job but I knew better than that. She never worked more than a short while and she wouldn't cook or clean very often which she agreed to do in exchange for me letting her stay in one of the bedrooms.

I said, no Tami, you will have to look for another place to stay because I am going to rent this place out to someone who will make the payments or sell it!

Around this time she moved a drug problem friend of hers and both of her two kids, a girl and a smaller boy, into the bedroom I allowed her to stay in. I told them to leave but she argued that I couldn't tell them to leave because she lived there and had invited them. See the law, what she said is true!

She asked for the house a few more times and each time I said no!

She started having more and more bums visit her and some were even hanging out in the front yard like they do on skid row. I told the ones in the yard to leave or I was calling the police and I told another one that I caught with a crack pipe in my living room to leave also, which they did, but they kept coming back from time to time.

As the home I was building became almost ready for me to move into she apparently became desperate and she, or they, formulated a plan.

I came home from working on the home at around 9:00 or 10:00 PM and grabbed a piece of KFC chicken, put it in the microwave and sat down for a few minutes of TV with the chicken and a glass of water before I had to go to sleep so I could work the next day.

Oh by the way; they had put a deadbolt on the bedroom door which required a key for anyone to get into the room. In my house! And, refused to take it off! Were drugs or other stuff going on in there?

Most likely!

The girl child came out of her room, got a piece of chicken, took one bite and threw the rest away. I stated to the girl, if you are going to get food then eat it, ok. And, the girl went back into the bedroom.

In a short while I heard a "whap", and a scream from the girl and the girls mother said shut up and go to sleep you have school in the morning.

Then another whap and a scream and the same from the mother, go to sleep!

I went back toward the bedroom and asked loudly "how can she go to sleep with you beating on her?" "You better stop abusing that child or I'm calling the child protective services on you!"

The next thing I knew the door flew open, Tami was poking me in the chest with her finger saying "you're going to jail, you're going to jail!" I asked, for what? And, I said, Get out, Annette take your kids and all of you get out!

This all occurred in January 2004 but really I guess I'm getting ahead of myself. You will read all about this in the motions and notices I filed with the court later in this book. To keep down some of the suspense I will add that I did go to jail that night; she lied to the judge and said she owned the house and got a restraining order keeping me off of my own property and she got control of my home and business files and records, everything about me, date of birth, social security numbers, computers – everything and used them to extort and defraud me. Then later she ended up in prison for drug running was released in three years and came back after me again and after my house, which is the case below. Wow! The things that happened to me because I let her stay in my home is “off the charts”, as they say. They’re unbelievable and I never would have imagined that this could happen to anyone in this country, but it did. The problem is, “U N J U S T I C E!” You’ll read more about what occurred in January 2004 later in the book.

Chapter 12

The Government has 6,500,000 official documents yet none of them protect your identity

Right now I am going to jump ahead to 2008.

In early 2008 Monica answered the phone and a lady who works for the city of Casa Grande said that I needed to pick up my dog license for my Pit Bull named Joker at the City Hall and Monica handed the phone to me. She and I confirmed that the application was in my name.

I don't live in Casa Grande and I don't own a dog named Joker, I told the lady.

She said she had called the phone number on the application, which was in my name, and someone answered and gave them this phone number. I asked what the address was on the license application since I didn't even live in the city limits. She told me and I realized that was the address where Tami and her gang lived.

We traced it down by going to the city hall and other places and filed a police report in Casa Grande for identity theft against Tami. Remember, she had control of everything about me for some time back in 2004, even how to sign my signature which was on many papers she controlled back then.

Our life had been nice and peaceful up until now. Keep in mind, Tami, the plaintiff in this case got out of prison in 2007 and we got some threatening calls from her that year but after telling her she better not call us anymore and that the phone was tapped and that she would have a problem, she left us alone, for awhile.

Then some guy in his early twenties shows up at out door late in the evening telling my wife that I was going to run off with his girlfriend Tami and threatening to kick my ass, he said, but when I heard the voices from my office where I was working I headed that direction and as I was getting close to the door I heard that statement and I chased him off the property threatening him with bodily harm.

Then we started getting phone calls, weird, threatening and vulgar. We reported them to the police, of course.

In 2004 Tami went to prison for drug running and her boyfriend stayed in the house.

In 2005 I evicted him for drugs, no payments and a dead dog on a chain and after a lot of repairs moved Monica's kids into the house.

In 2007 we moved the kids to a new home in town.

In early April 2008 Monica and I went to Alaska to a business property we owned there.

Later, in 2008, we sold the home, the one in this case, to a family out of Michigan with a good down payment and terms on the balance, and they were on their way to move in and escrow was set to close in a couple weeks.

We had Monica's son give the keys to the house that the family was buying to one of their family members.

The family member drove to the house to do work on it and there was a chain and lock on the gate with a sign that said, "If you want to contact the owner call Tami" and her phone number. She was criminally trying to steal the house!

He called the Michigan family and told the husband about it. Paul, the husband called Tami and in the conversation he told her that his wife was driving out and will be in Arizona in two days and that the house is due to close escrow on that day.

The courts will take anything a person files if it has the possibility of being a claim against anyone.

And, as you will see later in this case, Tami had a personal relationship with a judge and went to him and he told her what to file.

This is according to the papers she filed with the court as you will see later and according to the attorney I fired who got it directly from the judge.

According to the attorney, just lately, in February 2009, the judge said on the bench one day when only the judge, Tami (the plaintiff) and the attorney were there: perhaps I should withdraw from this case because of my personal relationship with the plaintiff – (what did he say, A personal relationship?) – And the judge only asked her if she objected and, of course she said no. Why would she object!

Now guess what, this judge is the judge in her case against me. How biased and prejudiced can you get?

When she found out the house was sold and the new owners were moving in and that it was due to close escrow in two days she ran to the court, her judge apparently, and filed a law suit and a Lis Pendens which is a notice of court action. She then took copies of this to the title agency to stop the close of escrow and stopped the whole thing.

The next thing she did was criminally break into the home, change out all the locks and was trying to move in. The neighbors saw her and called me. Naturally I told them to call the sheriffs' office the next time she showed up.

And I called a locksmith and had him go to the house and change all the locks and leave the keys with Monica's son Dan and they did.

There were several sheriff calls as you will see by the documents filed with the court in this case. She broke in more than once, brought three truck loads of junk and a gang of people and broke in again.

The sheriff was called and they arrived with guns drawn according to documents she filed in the court and cited her for criminal trespass.

And as you will see later, her judge told the court for the criminal trespass charges to dismiss the charges and they did.

The buyers from Michigan managed to move into the house but the escrow could never close because she claimed she owned the house.

Monica and I called the attorney referral service from Alaska and they gave us the name and phone number of an attorney in Casa Grande with years of experience.

We called him and he said he could handle it for us but that I needed to send him a check for $2,000.00 which I did and he filed a Notice of Appearance in the court on our behalf.

When we got home we met with the attorney and he said all we need to do if file an Election to Forfeit on her, which he did and it gave her 20 days to pay $17,600.00 which is what he determined she owed. How can she owe anything? She gave it all up, went to prison and charged me money and a truck to get rid of her!

She didn't respond to the Election to forfeit that she received but she did go and file bankruptcy which put a hold on anything until the Federal Bankruptcy Court could conclude her bankruptcy case.

Then we got a notice the bankruptcy was terminated by the bankruptcy court because she didn't follow through with papers required by the court.

Her time was up on the Election to forfeit and when I got the notice from the bankruptcy court I went to the attorney's office and said to him that we needed to file an Affidavit of Completion of Forfeiture which we did. Still no word from her!

It was set for trial by the judge so the attorney and the plaintiff met to exchange information.

They had a hearing, the three of them, as our attorney told us that we don't need to be there and said it would be a waste of time for us so we didn't go the fifty or so miles to the court that day.

That was the hearing we really should have been at. That was the one where the judge talked about his "personal relationship" with her and if I had seen him I would have objected. We were misled by our own attorney but I didn't know any of this at that time.

Then on September 9th, 2008 I am served with an Order from her judge that I cannot sell the home. And, as you will read in court documents that I filed, when he did this he notified me that he has already decided that she was the winner and I would have to give her the home.

How can he do that before there has been a trial? He can't! By doing so he showed his bias and prejudice and that he had already ruled in her favor and there had not even been a trial. Basically, he said, guilty without a trial. That's not legal! But he did it!

The trial came and lasted from 10:00 AM to 4:00 PM and at the end the judge said he was going to rule that she gets the house and I owed her money on top of the house.

So what do I have here? I have a drug addict that I tried to help out trying to steal a home I own; a judge that, according to the attorney had a personal relationship with her so he is perhaps biased and prejudiced against me; and, I have a lawyer that is inefficient and didn't even attempt to win the case. So, as you will see in the following documents that I filed with the court, I fired the attorney and would try to handle the case myself.

The reason I have to handle it myself is because I contacted every attorney in Casa Grande and they said they cannot represent me because the plaintiff had contacted them and it would be a conflict of interest. Wow, I can't even get a lawyer! She talked to everyone that I called before I did. But none of them are representing her and yet because they talked to her, they can't represent me!

Chapter 13

Lawyers do not represent you in any court action! They only represent the amount of money you have to pay them!

The following is the first page of notice I filed with the court:

IN THE SUPERIOR COURT OF THE STATE OF ARIZONA

IN AND FOR THE COUNTY OF PINAL

	)	**No. CV200801499**
	)	
Plaintiff,	)	**Assigned to Hon. Robert**
	)	**Carter Olson,**
v.	)	**Division 9**
	)	
	)	**NOTICE OF**
	)	**TERMINATION OF**
Defendant.	)	**SERVICES BY**
	)	**ATTORNEY HOWARD**
	)	**K** xxxx
	)	**AND REQUEST FOR**
	)	**NEW TRIAL**

Defendant, in Pro Per, moves the court to accept the termination of the services rendered by Counsel Howard K xxxx **on behalf of the Defendant for inadequate and inefficient representation and to grant Defendant a new trial by another Judge.**

GROUNDS – I submitted five pages of reasons to fire the attorney and for a new judge

Chapter 14

"If you don't read the newspaper, you are uninformed. If you do read the newspaper, you are misinformed. .... Mark Twain"

Of course I never did get an answer from the court regarding this notice until the hearing that was scheduled for February 13th, 2009.

I did however get a ruling/order from the court around the time I filed the termination notice.

He issued the ruling/order on December 5, 2008.

The judge ruled that I have to give her the house; I have to give her credit for any payments I have made on the house since 2005; and, that I owe her $14,560.00 plus interest at 7.375 per annum from March 23, 2005.

He did however rule that it is not a final order subject to superior claims by any third party and that the matter is set for status review on February 13, 2009.

Let me give you a little advice based on research, talking to others regarding court issues and personal experience; if you don't have a lot of money you are much better off fighting any, and I repeat, any court action without an attorney! But, you need to know about the Rules of Court and some about the law. I will discuss more about that later.

Another thing that occurred apparently on the 5th of December was the plaintiff somehow got a copy that day. Of course I didn't and on the 8th of December, Monday, I had to go to the courthouse and ask for a copy.

I actually found out about it on the 6th of December, Saturday, but I wasn't able to read it and didn't get a copy of it.

On the 6th of December the plaintiff and some of her gang showed up at the home and according to the family who live there, from Michigan, threatened them apparently by saying that they would blow their heads off and she told them to get out of her house. The sheriff was called by the family.

One of the officers put handcuffs on the plaintiff and put her in the back seat of his car and was going to arrest her. The second officer didn't say or do anything.

Another officer showed up and talked to her and told the first officer to let her go, apparently, as he did and the four of them talked for awhile by the car.

The officer told the family that they had told her to leave and showed the Notice/Order above but said it wasn't a final order. They also told the family that they needed to go to court and get an Injunction against Harassment, which they did on Monday the 8th of December so we went with the lady, Suzanne, to the justice court.

The plaintiff was also at the court but left before we did.

After getting the Injunction Suzanne left to go home which was west and Monica and I decided we were going the other way, east, to have breakfast at I-Hop on Florence Blvd.

This is spooky as she must have been stalking or following us.

We left the courthouse and went east on Cottonwood and turned south on Peart Road.

When we arrived at the intersection of Florence Blvd. and Peart Rd. we got in the left turn lane and stopped for the red light.

Monica was in the passenger seat with her window mostly down and I was driving with my window partly down.

When we stopped we saw a white vehicle with black stripes pulling up in the right lane and it contained the plaintiff and another female passenger.

The plaintiff was looking directly at Monica and I and her passenger was also looking in our direction. The passengers' face was partly hidden behind the head of the plaintiff so I didn't get a clear view of who she was.

The plaintiff yelled over to us "I'm gonna fu-- you up bi-ch!" The passenger said I'm gonna back her up. The plaintiff flipped her middle finger toward us and they turned right heading west on Florence Blvd.

Monica dialed 911 and the light turned green so I turned east. Both Monica and I have an Order of Protection against the plaintiff as she has numerous times threatened to kill us. We were asked by the 911 operator to wait at one of the businesses in the area and we advised her that we would be in the CVS Pharmacy parking lot and we proceeded there.

A city police officer arrived and took down the report and the

Protection order number and said they would proceed with it from there.

The good thing about this, even though she is dangerous and could hurt or kill someone is, they have her scheduled for trial on these criminal charges but the bad thing is, they ended up dismissing them for lack of evidence.

The plaintiff and her gang are dangerous. Almost all of them have extensive criminal backgrounds and the plaintiff herself just got out of Federal Prison in 2007 for drugs and related criminal activity.

If you don't believe how dangerous she is read what she did to me in January 2004 and review the many police involved incidents with the plaintiff. She was trying to kill me!

In addition they have been seen by several people including Monica and I shooting AK-47's and other firearms in the yard. And the plaintiff has stated that those guys will kill for me (her). They are dangerous and someone is going to get killed if she isn't stopped.

The problem is the sheriffs' officers are not doing anything about it. They keep saying it's a civil matter, no one has been hurt yet and they keep letting her go!

Then, on December 12th, 2008 the plaintiff and some of her gang showed up at the home again even though she knew she had Orders of Protection and Injunction against Harassment and was told to stay away from Suzanne's family and us.

One of them actually walked up to the door and left a paper on the door telling Suzanne and Paul to move in five days.

The sheriff was called and they said "it's a civil matter" and didn't do anything.

On the 16th of December I got up and my cell phone beeped so I checked messages and there was a message saying "Mr. Turney… ….Monica's dead!"

On the 17th of December Paul and Suzanne were served a notice to appear in the local justice court for an eviction process by a process server. We filed an answer on the 22nd and in court on the 23rd the judge referred it back to the same judge that the plaintiff knows.

After we left the court on the 23rd we were driving down John Wayne Parkway in the city of Maricopa where the courthouse is and she (Tami) tried to ram us. The sheriff was called and they wouldn't do anything.

As I have said elsewhere in this book the Rules of Court are more important to the judges than Justice or a Fair Trial. That's "unjustice"! Since I am rapidly becoming aware of that, I am trying to study the law since lawyers aren't efficient and the courts, as Solomon says, are corrupt.

I remembered reading recently in the court rules that I have to file a Notice of Change of Address since I fired the attorney and all mail was going to him, if there was any.

So, on December 29, 2008 I filed a notice of change of address. If you don't do that they can send the mail anywhere, I guess, and you lose because you didn't reply to whatever document was sent, that you didn't get, within the time limit by the court rules.

And, on December 30, 2008 I filed the Notice of Superior Claims as the judge stated in his Notice/Order dated on December 5,

2008, which took several days to prepare.

Please forgive the repetitiveness of some of the statements. That is because of “unjustice”! If you file it once and they dismiss it you can’t use the document or evidence attached in a different motion. You have to repeat it in the next motion because the prior motion was dismissed and can’t be used again except possibly in an appeal.

NOTE: Any exhibit numbers shown in the documents submitted may not be the same as the exhibits in other court documents filed. The reason for this is the Rules of Court.

If I had actually placed the exhibits for each and every motion or notice in this book it probably would have been at least 2,000 pages long. Of course, I had to keep filing exhibits with each new motion or notice and it was necessary to renumber them as some were appropriate and some were inappropriate for each different motion or notice.

.

Chapter 15

"Government is the great fiction, through which everybody endeavors to live at the expense of everybody else. .... Frederic Bastiat, French Economist (1801-1850)"

Notice of Superior Claims follows:

IN THE SUPERIOR COURT OF THE STATE OF ARIZONA

IN AND FOR THE COUNTY OF PINAL

	)	**No. CV200801499**
	)	
Plaintiff,	)	**Assigned to Hon. Robert Carter Olson Division 9**
	)	
v.	)	
	)	
	)	
	)	**NOTICE OF SUPERIOR CLAIMS**
Defendant.	)	
	)	
	)	

DEFENDANT **in Pro Per submits to the Court prima facia evidence that there are SUPERIOR CLAIMS stated on many occasions in the Court Notice/Order dated 12/05/2008 and as proven in testimony and evidence at trial and asks the Court to recognize prior superior claims.**

SUPERIOR CLAIMS

SUPERIOR CLAIM 1: CITI MORTGAGE.

This Court is aware of the third-party claim(s) which are superior to all claims in this litigation who is Citi Mortgage and Citi Mortgage has stated that they will enforce their Deed of Trust and place the property in foreclosure for violation of page 10 term 18 and through contact with Citi's Legal Department, should anyone issue an order giving the property to anyone else, according to Branch Manager Chad and Customer Service Representative Noah.

Should the Court make a Final Judgment and Order the Defendant to give possession of the property to the Plaintiff the Court would be ordering the Defendant to Violate the Deed of Trust with Citi Mortgage.

Plaintiff recorded, four years after the fact, in the Pinal County Recorders Office the document which would subject the property to foreclosure action. The Agreement was never intended by either party to be recorded or intended as a sale agreement. It was only intended to be a rental agreement with many terms and conditions that were agreed to by both parties and at the end of 30

years would be a sale (Note: see "Superior Claim 3 for the explanation as to how this occurred – by EXTORTION, which wasn't allowed to be admitted into evidence in this Court.). After conversation with Citi Mortgage in December 2008 it has been determined that the Agreement did in fact violate the terms of the Deed of Trust as it did transfer ownership at a future date. However, since a Notice of Termination of the Agreement was recorded in the Pinal County Recorders Office and the violation of the Deed of Trust terminated by that action foreclosure for violation of the Deed of Trust could be avoided.

The Plaintiff in this matter was just recently in Bankruptcy proceedings and most likely cannot qualify to Citi Mortgage or another finance company to pay off the mortgage to Citi Mortgage and now that the Defendant is aware that the Agreement is a violation of the Deed of Trust refuses to enter any such agreement now or in the future unless ordered to do so.

The plaintiff, continues to this day to ignore the law and violate and threaten anyone who gets in her way and to manipulate the courts for her own gain and are assisted by many of the people she associates with. The Court should note the following damage to the property complaints, Orders of Protection and Injunctions against Harassment against the Plaintiff just since early 2008:

Injunction of Harassment, to stop threatening with death and harassing the family;

Order of Protection against Plaintiff to stop threatening the Defendant and his wife;

The Court should be aware of the Plaintiff's illegal activity against the property, the Defendant, his wife and the family as indicated by the City Of Casa Grande Police Reports and Pinal County Sheriff's Office Reports.

SUPERIOR CLAIM 2:

In fact, there is a second superior third-party claim to the property which is the family who started a purchase of the property on March 29, 2008 which was placed into escrow and in which they had paid a non-refundable $10,000.00 down payment and had paid the first monthly payment and was to pay an additional $20,000.00 toward the down payment on or before September 1, 2008.

This was prior to any claim by Tami and prior to the Plaintiff recording the four year old (2004) Agreement to which the Defendant immediately recorded the Notice of Violation and Right to Evict as agreed in the terms of the 2004 Agreement and the Eviction Notice as agreed by Plaintiff in the Agreement.

To the best of Defendants knowledge, a suit against Defendant does not stop the sale of property. It only puts everyone on notice that there is pending litigation against the Defendant not only that but it was claimed after the sale was initiated.

Sometime later, the family notified the Defendant that they would not be able to pay the additional $20,000.00 as agreed which could subject them to the loss of any money paid and forfeiture of the property to the Defendant. They asked the Defendant to give them more time with a Rent To Own Agreement which the Defendant found himself feeling bad that they would lose the money they had paid toward the property plus the Defendant needed the payments they had agreed to pay each month so that he, Defendant, could make the payments to Citi Mortgage and agreed to enter a Rent To Own agreement with the family which was dated September 1, 2008.

The Defendant consented to a Rent To Own Agreement with the family as long as they would acknowledge in the Agreement that they were aware of the suit by Plaintiff and they were informed that they should not do any repairs or upgrades to the property until the issue was settled, however, they have spent thousands of dollars on the home and property with new carpeting, new hardwood flooring, new windows, new sliding door, trees, landscaping, a new back deck and cover and more. They have been in the home with possession since April 2008.

In September Defendant's Counsel gave Defendant a Notice or Order by the Court dated 09/09/2008 to not sell the property and Defendant gave Counsel a copy of the Sales Agreement and the Rent to Own Agreement with the family, dated 9/1/2008 which was prior to this order, for Counsel to give to the Court and for his information.

This transaction, with the family, was concluded prior to the Order from the Court and prior to the conversations with Citi Mortgage in December 2008 wherein Citi Mortgage said it would be a violation of their Deed of Trust but if the purchaser could get a new loan from them it would not be.

The family has shown that they have a very good credit rating and in fact will and have qualified to finance and pay off the mortgage to Citi Mortgage.

In fact if the Defendant did not receive the monthly payments from the family for rent on the property in this matter the Defendant would not be able to make the payments on the property and it would be in foreclosure.

Should the Court order the property be given to Plaintiff the property will go into foreclosure for failure to pay because the

Defendant cannot pay the payments without the income from the family's rent payments.

SUPERIOR CLAIM 3: THE DEFENDANT.

The Defendant has a right to protect the property from the Plaintiff and an Obligation to protect the interest of Citi Mortgage as the Defendant is indebted to Citi Mortgage by the Deed of Trust and Note for the property and in fact only entered into the Agreement with Plaintiff because of threats and extortion.

The Defendant would offer to the Court the following brief story about how the Plaintiff gained possession of the property from the Defendant. None of this was allowed to be presented to the Court. This is a very short version but there were many more things that occurred because of Plaintiff's drug use:

Defendant met the Plaintiff when she was a hostess in Cottonwood Arizona and after she picked him up at the bar, after she ascertained in conversations and his use of an American Express card to pay the bill where she worked, and after spending the night in his hotel room and her girlfriend in the room of Defendants partner, that he was a successful business man, she soon pursued the Defendant by moving to Phoenix and near Defendants business where she said that she went to work as a hostess. Defendant was 46 and he found out later, she was 20 years old.

The Defendant worked 7 days a week in his business but was always full of energy and thought he was in love. Little did Defendant know that to get him, the Defendant, to marry her, the Plaintiff was putting cocaine in his coffee every morning and night without his knowledge but Defendant thought he was in love, he was full of energy and within a month after meeting married her not knowing that the good feelings toward her were the drugs she was putting in his coffee. A few years later she confessed to putting cocaine in his coffee morning and night.

Within two weeks Defendant caught Plaintiff, a girl friend of hers who was only 15 and her 25 year old boyfriend in bed at the house the Defendant had rented but after denying that she had done anything, the Defendant didn't divorce her.

In a month the Defendant found out that Plaintiff was pregnant and had an abortion and the doctor told the Defendant that she had gotten pregnant in the first or second week of June which was when Defendant caught them in bed together.

Then Plaintiff confessed and informed the Defendant of her cocaine addiction and asked him to help her get off the drug(s) and confessed that she worked at a nude dance club for the money to support her drug addiction which she claimed she got from her bosses, Jim and Martin.

After Defendant found out about her drug problem he told her to stop or that he would divorce her and she did stop for some time.

Within a short time she, the Plaintiff, filed for a divorce, so she could go back to work at the nude dance club and get cocaine from her boss there, she said.

Defendant felt sorry for Plaintiff, told her to live her life the way she wants and she stopped the divorce. In time she grew tired of that lifestyle and asked the Defendant to again help her, so she could get off drugs, which Defendant did and then after a year or so she got back on cocaine and crystal meth and went back to work at the nude peek show club. During this time period she admitted to the Defendant that she was putting cocaine in his coffee when they first met.

Defendant couldn't take any more and divorced her in 1994 after catching her in a motel room with another man and her brother Jimmy all together. This occurred one time, after many such times, when she had disappeared for several days but this time her horse was sick and dying in the pasture. I called one of her friends, Rana and told her about the horse and asked if she had seen Tami and she told me that she had saw Tami's car in front of Room 1 at the Truck Stop Motel on I-8. When I got there Tami's car was there so I knocked on the door and stepped back to the window and when she opened the curtain to see who was at the door, she was naked, the guy was pulling up his pants and Jimmy, her brother, was still in the bed. So I filed and got the divorce.

During the divorce she wanted the café and store that I owned and she agreed to pay me for the inventory if I would give

them to her. The place didn't make any money and I was happy to get rid of it, even though we had a pre-nuptial agreement, so I told her she would only have to pay me for the inventory. We pulled an inventory and she gave Defendant a note for $30,000.00, for the inventory.

Local people complained to Defendant that the Plaintiff and some of her friends were dealing drugs out of the cafe and in fact one of her cooks was killed in or near Superior Arizona around that time and according to the newspapers it was a drug related crime. His name was Garret or Garrett but I forget his last name.

In four to six months Plaintiff called the Defendant and said that Defendant could have the store and café back, because she couldn't pay the bills. Defendant drove to the store with a lady in his car by the name of Gail and when we pulled up in the parking lot Tami, Plaintiff, came running out and threatened to kill Gail so we left and Gail had me drive her to the Casa Grande Justice Court and she took out an Order of Protection on Tami which was not contested by Tami, Plaintiff.

In a week or so Defendant received a final notice for an electric bill for over $6,000.00 from APS which was for the store and café, the account was still in his name, so he called her and went to the store which was closed but Tami was there. She said you can have it back, threw the keys at him and drove away in her

car. He went in and the inventory was totally gone, there was nothing left in the store or café to sell, just empty space, she had sold it all!

I paid the bills and re-stocked the store and café and in a couple days was driving by late in the evening and low and behold Tami, her mother Norma K and father Tim K and her sister Sandra M and two men were all coming out of my store with bags of groceries and the truck bed was full. I had neglected to change the locks! I ordered them off the property but they wouldn't leave so I called the Sheriff's Office. When an officer arrived I told him what happened but the Plaintiff lied and claimed she owned the store and café. The officer told all of us to leave and to take it up in civil court. The next morning Defendant changed the locks.

In 1995 or 1996 she came crying back to me saying she lost her place to live and wanted to move into one of the rooms at my house. After saying no, several times, Defendant reluctantly told her not to move in very much because it will not work out and that she better not bring any drugs to his house. Her sister Sandra M and her boyfriend Larry came by my house before Tami had moved anything into it. They were on their way back to live in Kingman. They sold me some videos and a bedroom set which I bought because they needed the money to make the move and just before they left they told me, because they were mad at Tami at the time, these are her sister Sandra's words, not mine, "don't sleep

with her, she has been fu--ing every nig--- in Casa Grande, dealing drugs, prostituting and shooting drugs!"

She stayed at my house and would clean it sometime and cook at times and appeared to be off drugs. We didn't live as husband and wife and I wouldn't sleep with her because of my knowledge of what she was and drug abuse.

At one time she asked me to write her a letter saying she got paid for working for me and I said that I would not do that. She was trying to buy a car or something and needed something to show income. I said well you are staying at my house free with free utilities that amounts to about a thousand dollars a month you don't have to pay out. She said to write something for $1,300.00 a month and as a second thought asked me to say it was a gift so she could get the car or for welfare or some other reason I am unaware of. Defendant complied with her wishes and she got a car but within a few months lost it because she couldn't make the payments.

The Plaintiff appeared to the Defendant to be off drugs and we were getting along fairly well for a while and occasionally we would go to her mother and father's house in Kingman Arizona to visit for a day or two.

On one visit her mother and father were re-confirming their marriage vows in Laughlin Nevada and we were there and Tami, Plaintiff, tried to get me to re-marry her while we were there but I said, no Tami!

Another time we were at their house and her brother Jimmy and her sister Laurie and her sister Sandy all got into an argument and somehow I was drawn into it. Jimmy said he was going to kick my ass and said step outside. When we got outside he kept walking toward the entrance to the driveway instead of stopping in the clear area outside the door. There was a block fence at the entrance and when he got to it he turned to face me and was ready to fight but obviously wanted me to hit him first. I'm not big on fighting, I was a lot older than him and he was in better physical shape and out of the corner of my left eye I saw movement and there was their sister Laurie stooped down with a chrome pistol in her hand. I walked away and got in my car and Tami, the Plaintiff, jumped in as I was driving off and asked why I didn't hit him and I just said it wasn't worth it. They had it set up to kill me that time! Tami, the Plaintiff, denied any knowledge or involvement.

She kept pushing to re-marry and I said no every time! We didn't sleep together, I just felt sorry for her and tried to help her, but in any case I wouldn't marry her!

In March 2002 I bought a manufactured home, the one she now is trying to claim is hers, from Stamey's manufactured home lot in Casa Grande and put it on property I owned.

Defendant let Plaintiff move into her own room and because he felt sorry for her and she seemed to still be clean of drugs he was willing to try to help her. Defendant was going to, later, rent out this manufactured home or sell it when the home he was building on the lot next door was completed.

In 2003 the Defendant had some money from selling a lot that he owned and a little more that he had put aside to finish the house next door so he went to work on it seven days a week and several times hired contractors for some of it.

One day when Defendant walked in he went directly to the kitchen sink to wash up and looked through the opening and saw one of Plaintiffs friends, Kim trying to hide something from him in the couch. He asked, "What's that?" and she held it up, it was a crack/meth pipe and he told her to get out of my house and she said "It's ok with Tami" and I said, "it's not, get out!" Tami was in her bedroom at the time, I guess, as they had put a deadbolt on the bedroom door so no one could get in without a key which allowed the drug use to go on in one of the Defendants bedroom, behind his back.

Then she let Annette and her two kids move in and when I found out I told them to leave but Tami, the Plaintiff, said that I can't make them leave and since I was near to finishing the house next door I didn't fight it even though I did tell her twice to take her kids and leave my house because of her being high.

By January 2004 I had the home almost completely built and Tami stated "when you move over there, I want this house!" meaning the manufactured home to which, I responded, no! You can't make the payments! You don't even work! You're going to need to find another place to live because I am going to rent this one out to pay the bills or sell it if I can find a buyer who can come up with their own financing to pay it off! And of course also because of her drug problem.

On January 11, 2004 I came home from working on the house next door and they (Tami and Annette) were beating Annette's daughter in Tami's bedroom. I yelled at them to stop beating that girl and told all of them to get out of my house. They rushed out of the bedroom and Tami stuck her finger in my chest and said "you're going to jail"! "For what", I asked. I said, "All of you get out!" Annette told her daughter to take the boy and go to the car. We all went to the front porch where I stopped just outside the door, on the porch. Tami was in front of me and Annette and the kids were at their car. Annette was calling someone and said on the phone something along the lines of send the police, Mac is

beating up Tami. I looked at her and all of a sudden things went black, Tami had knocked me out but I heard the glass of water that I was drinking hit the floor and I pushed her away. Apparently I pushed her or she jumped off the porch to the ground. Annette was saying hurry, I assume to the 911 operator and I looked toward her. I seen movement out of my left eye and instinctively stuck up my left hand. Something hit it HARD and it felt broken. I heard something slam down on the porch…whatever she hit me with had broken. I looked at my hand and grabbed it with my right hand, it hurt. Then I saw movement toward my head again…but I was too late…everything went black. The next thing I know is I was trying to lock the door from the inside of the house and the Plaintiff was pushing on it trying to get in. I got it locked and shortly thereafter the police showed up while I was in the bathroom looking at my head, face, hand, arms and legs…they were all cut and bruised. She apparently beat me unconscious with something and was trying to kill me.

Needless to say…two women saying that I had hit Tami is a lost battle long before it gets started in any court in America. She said she was hurt and went off in an ambulance and I was taken to jail and I am certain the booking photo will show a lot of blood on me even though the officer gave me a wet towel to clean it off so he could take the photo. She was charged also but got out, went to my home and managed to keep me out of my own home.

The officer's statement confirms that the Defendant was the Victim. It confirms that Defendant was beaten with a "stick" according to the Plaintiff, but it confirms that the Defendant was hit with an object that the Plaintiff was not born with. It also says the Defendant was intoxicated.

The Defendant was not intoxicated, he was semi-conscious from being hit in the head! If the officer took a test to determine the alcohol level of the Defendant he does not remember it but he is certain it would not show more than the level of 2 beers which he had drank several hours earlier when he stopped work on the house next door. He was not intoxicated! He had just been knocked out once at the door by the Plaintiff! He was again knocked out and severely beaten with a rake by the Plaintiff. Plaintiff later admitted it was a rake! The Defendant was in shock and a state of semi-consciousness! The Plaintiff tried to beat him to death with the rake and even chased him into the house trying to finish the job. Plaintiff and Annette conspired to do great bodily harm to the Defendant and have him arrested for starting the fight as evidenced by threats in the hall before they went outside and by the phone call to 911 by Annette prior to the Plaintiff knocking the Defendant out the first time. Actually the beating by the Plaintiff was Assault with a Deadly Weapon and if it were a man he would have been so charged, photos of Defendant taken a few days later.

The Plaintiff actually started in January 2004 trying to usurp the Defendants home when she told the police and obviously the Judge or someone in authority that she owned the home and the Judge upon release would not let the Defendant return to his own home.

The next morning at around 9Am I went before a Judge Goodman, I assume, at the jail and he released me but said I could not go back to my house. I explained that I owned it and that I was letting the Plaintiff stay in a room in my house. He said that she said it was her house, and he asked if I was going to go back to the house and he stated that if I was going back there that he wasn't going to let me out! I accepted the terms and had a friend pick me up and stayed at his home in Scottsdale while I tried to figure out how to get those people out of my house and heal from the beating. I took the photographs within a couple days but some of the damage had healed by then. The Plaintiff had control of my office, my computers, files, papers and documents and everything I owned including my home! I was still in post traumatic stress. After a few weeks I moved into the home I had been working on next door even though it wasn't finished.

The Plaintiff had possession of everything Defendant owned including all of my business records, files and computers. She had the names and addresses of every business contact and all of their information. She had control of my life because someone ordered

me not to go back to my own home; the home I had bought which was in my name only and Defendant wasn't married to anyone.

Defendant made arrangements with a court order for an officer to go with me to get some of my things but the officer said that she only had a few minutes so I needed to make it quick. I would end up with very few items and the officer and I had to go. The Plaintiff still had possession of 90% of my property and almost all of my business information.

Defendant hired an attorney Pamela A to help me deal with all of the false claims by the Plaintiff. We were working on this when the Plaintiff contacted me and said she had hit me with a rake and that "it's a good thing that you took the plea bargain like I did because the County Attorney said he was going to have your ass and prosecute you to the fullest." And, she tried to get me to feel sorry for her again and asked for the house and she said, if I would give it to her that I could have my stuff, but I didn't fall for it and I knew that Attorney A would get my home and property back.

The plaintiff knew that she couldn't possibly convince anyone that she had any claim to the home and property: she was not the Defendants wife, she was just being allowed use of a room in the home of the Defendant while he was trying to help her stay off drugs but obviously she had started using drugs again and

everyone she associated with were drug addicts and her name had never been on the title to the home. Plaintiff knew that she had to do something or she was going to loose her free place to stay; the Defendant had already told her she was going to need to find another place to live when he moved and she couldn't talk him into renting it to her – no job, no income, drugs and drug addict friends, etc., so she had to take it into her own hands somehow. Apparently she or they formulated a plan.

Then the Plaintiff contacted the Defendant again and began EXTORTION by saying that she had every name, address and phone numbers for Defendants business contacts and customers and all of my records and my computer and files and tax records and that if the Defendant didn't give her the house that she would contact all of them and would harass them to the point that they would stop using the Defendant for any of their work and that she would destroy everything of the Defendants, before he could get it all back. She also said that Mark S, a neighbor, was a computer hacker and they had already sent out emails from my computer using my name and account and that they had messed with my computer, files and copied all of my information. And, that wasn't all they were going to do if Defendant didn't give her the house and property. To this day I do not know what they did with all my computer information and who they sent emails to or what they did to that computer and my files and customers.

So, in May 2004 the EXTORTION worked as Plaintiff, on top of the threats above, threatened to sue the Defendant for getting hurt when she, in her words, was pushed off the porch and was transported to the hospital and claimed her back was hurt on the defendant's property.

And, she pushed the EXTORTION harder because now she had piled all of the Defendants stuff on the back porch, in the rain, which would ruin all the files, records, computers, papers and books plus one of the couches and a chair so we entered into what the wording says is a Real Estate Offer and Purchase Agreement which is the only way that she would accept it even though the Defendant tried to word it as a Rental Agreement with many terms and conditions that would prove that it is only a rental agreement and the Defendant figured that she couldn't live by it anyway because she didn't work, she didn't have any money and had no income, she had drug problems and more. That was the only way the Defendant could get back all of his personal property, business files and records and his computer and get them out of the rain and to stop her from contacting customers and totally ruining the business.

It was obvious to the Defendant that the Sheriff's Officers and County Attorney at the time and the Justice System was of no value in protecting him and that Tami S K, Plaintiff, could get them to do anything for her and against the Defendant and they

even allowed her to gain possession of everything he owned and ordered him to stay out of his own home.

Tami, Plaintiff, had already proven that she could control the Defendants life with the manipulation of the Officers and the Justice System and had in fact gained full control of everything the Defendant owned since January 11, 2004 because of lies and getting a Judge to issue a restraining order against him by saying she owned the home even though her name was never on the home as an owner and they weren't married.

As further evidence that the Plaintiff by Extortion forced the Defendant to enter into the Agreement dated May 24, 2004 which is the matter before this Court.

The Plaintiff was, at the same time that she had possession and control of the Defendants home, business, phones and everything he owned, after she beat him severely with a rake and conspired with Annette to frame him for starting the fight, threatened Defendant that she was going to file suit against him for getting hurt on his property.

When the Defendant agreed to sign an Agreement on the house, under duress by Extortion, the Plaintiff put some plastic over his stuff on the porch and she voluntarily gave the document to the Defendant stating that she "will not sue Mac Turney" which

released another one of her Extortion threats that she was using to get the Defendant to do whatever she wanted. And, she allowed him to get his stuff that was on the back porch out of the rain but a lot of it had been destroyed.

The Plaintiff made a couple payments as shown in the Court and kept promising to pay what she owed. She said she had a good job that paid her cash to haul construction equipment all over the U. S. and that she should be able to keep up the rent payments. Her, her friends and a bunch of people I had never seen before kept coming and going from my house for months with trucks, trailers, cars and assorted vehicles.

During the next several months she kept telling Defendant that she was getting paid for hauling construction equipment but they still owed her and will pay her soon and that she will pay the rent payments soon. Of course, Defendant was uncertain of what she could do with the threats, involved with his own life and let her slide for some time.

Some time in early 2005 she went to jail but at the time the Defendant did not know that it was for drug trafficking and that she was arrested in Kentucky. Her boyfriend Fabian O kept telling Defendant that he would get the money to pay the rent payments because he had a construction job going and would get paid when it

was done so again the Defendant let it slide for some more time.

When Plaintiff showed up at my house in mid 2005 with $20,000.00 toward payments, back charges and the balance of $10,000.00 to be decided by me once I was able to retrieve the payment history and to apply it as appropriate, I accepted it and gave her a receipt. Defendant knew it wasn't all that she owed and he gave instructions that she better keep the terms of the agreement in the future. He also suspected the money wasn't from hauling construction equipment and tried to contact someone at DEA to report it but stopped out of concern over the threats.

Later the Defendant found out that she had been in jail for money laundering and drug related charges and that the vehicles they were arrested in (her, Patricia B and several other people) were the same vehicles they were driving from his property (the house in this matter) because after she was released from jail in mid 2005 the same vehicles were coming and going and kept showed up again and later she told the Defendant that they were the same vehicles they were arrested in back in Kentucky but the DEA had given them back to her.

She went back to jail which Defendant understood was for a drug use violation. The home had been trashed but now it got worse, windows broken, roof torn off, junk in yard, old vehicles,

dead dog on a chain tied to a tree and more, with people coming and going all night and day.

Finally after seeing the trashed situation the Defendant went to her boyfriend Fabian and told him to clean up the place and do the repairs as needed and to start taking care of their animals or the Defendant would evict him as Tami, the Plaintiff is in violation of the agreement.

Not long after that he and all his friends packed up things and left. They didn't come back!

Shortly after that the Defendant was contacted by, I believe, Patricia B's daughter Anna, so they could get into the house and pack and store all of Tami's stuff in a Mobile Mini unit and move it to Richard's house because Tami was going to be in prison for three years, they said. So, I let them do that! Her own witnesses in the Court prove they moved her stuff and abandoned the home.

Afterward, the place was abandoned and falling apart. I posted a notice of violation on the house and evicted an empty house and used the notice to notify her friends who were still coming around, after they violated every term in the agreement and the home was falling apart. The house was getting broken into by her friends, even with the notice on the door and gate and they were leaving drug paraphernalia laying around and doing a lot of

damage to the place. After we did extensive repairs to the place, new windows and doors, screens, cleaned the carpet twice to get out the stink from animals, cats, dogs, ferrets, birds and more, painted and fixed the rooms and removed all the junk from the yard which cost several thousand dollars we put our son and daughter in the house as caretakers and we paid the utilities to keep the place from getting destroyed and burned down by drug addicts which in doing so cost Defendant $760.00 a month for caretakers.

Defendant had some contact with the Plaintiff but at a distance because she had made threats to him and extorted the Defendant and he knew that she could use the court system to get what she wanted. He didn't know what she was capable of doing but it was obvious that the Plaintiff and Patricia B could manipulate the Courts and end up only getting three years, when the men involved got 35 years to life, and they could have got the same sentence. It was already obvious that Plaintiff could manipulate officers and the courts in this area too and that the Defendant would be the one in trouble. Plaintiff even made a threat to kill the Defendant by saying "those guys will kill for me", while pointing toward Fabian and three or four other guys in the yard and that a certain friend of hers, Greg, Gums as he is known, would kill anyone for her if she just told him to.

No one ever made any payments to the mortgage company other than the Defendant! And, he continues to make the payments to Citi Mortgage to this day! The mortgage is in the Defendants name only and always has been.

Lo and Behold after all these years the Plaintiff decides to usurp the house after violating all the terms, abandoning it for years and not making the payments and recording a four year old document that the Plaintiff, <u>with malice</u> <u>by threats and extortion forced the Defendant to enter into,</u> which was written as a Rental Agreement with clauses that allowed her to buy it if she paid the payments for 30 years and didn't violate the other terms of the agreement such as trashing it, letting it fall apart, not making payments, not using it for illegal use, etc. Plaintiff violated many of the terms of the Agreement! PLUS, THE PLAINTIFF AND ALL OF HER WITNESSES ADMITTED ON THE WITNESS STAND IN THE COURT THAT THEY WERE USING THE HOME FOR UNLAWFUL ACTIVITY INCLUDING DRUG AND MONEY LAUNDERING!, which this Court ignored. Defendant thought any Court would recognize all the terms of an Agreement and that the Agreement which includes EVERY TERM within it would be upheld by any Court.

In return Defendant recorded the second eviction notice that was posted at the house in 2006 Fee Number: 2008-052071, just a few days after Plaintiff recorded the (4) four year old

agreement that was null and void in his best judgment and gotten by Extortion.

Later, in 2007, to satisfy threats by Plaintiff, Defendant gave her a 1 ton dually he purchased for her for $8,500.00 and a check for $7,000.00 saying paid in full which she cashed (which is what she asked for) to terminate the 2004 Agreement, along with the hand written agreement that she made stating that this was payment in full for any claims she may have against the Defendant forever.

(See <u>more regarding the truck</u> towing a car that was used in a <u>Homicide</u>.)

As criminal minded as the Plaintiff, Tami, is the Defendant knew better and should have never trusted that she would honor any agreement!

In 2008 Tami, Plaintiff, started trying to forcefully steal the property from Defendant and with a gang of her hoodlum friends showed up, cut the lock and chain off of the gate, burglarized the house and changed all of the locks but Officers have managed to temporarily keep her at bay but the threats of harm are real if she isn't stopped.

When it turned out that the Plaintiff couldn't forcefully take the house she started the Extortion all over again only this time with different threats.

Plaintiff called the Defendant while he was on vacation and threatened that he had better give her the house or she would take his business, claim that he cheated on his taxes, tell the real estate board that he was selling real estate without a license and claim that he was involved or had knowledge of the Drug Activity that the Plaintiff, Patricia B, Fabian O (by his own testimony before this Court) and others were involved in. All of which are lies and the Defendant wouldn't give her the house so she, the Plaintiff, has followed through with these threats by calling the IRS, the real estate board and by the Plaintiff and all of her witnesses committing perjury on the witness stand in this Court when they said under oath that the Defendant was aware or involved in their drug activity.

Defendant would like to point out to the Court that only the Plaintiff, Patricia B and others were arrested and convicted or pled guilty to the charges. Richard's involvement is unknown but Fabian O avoided the arrest somehow and yet he stated on the witness stand that the Defendant was aware of <u>their</u> drug activity. Note, he cleared the Defendant and left him out of involvement by saying that the Defendant "was aware of what <u>we</u> were doing" in a

separate statement, therefore admitting his guilt but he has never charged for these crimes, yet.

Plaintiff to this day continues to try to extort the Defendant!

And to this day, after trying to help her over and over get off drugs and clean up her life and giving her a place to stay and eventually divorcing her 15 years ago, she continues to try to extort money from Defendant, usurp his home and extort him into giving her everything he has worked all his life to acquire, his retirement. Defendant is 65 years old. Defendant has recorded threats of extortion from both Tami, Plaintiff, and her brother Calvin wherein they are demanding that he better give her the home and property or they have social security numbers and will make claims to the IRS and other threats, which they left on the answering machine identifying themselves with the time and date from the phone company, Qwest, on the recording and their phone numbers.

And now Plaintiff has Defendant in court over his house before the same County Attorney who, according to Tami said, "it's a good thing that you took the plea bargain like I did because the County Attorney said he was going to have your ass and prosecute you to the fullest." I swear that is what she said and if I can find the tapes of some of her conversations during 2004 I will give them to the Court! This was when she beat the Defendant with the rake in

January 2004 and claimed ownership of the home long before she extorted the Defendant into giving her an Agreement proving she schemed to get the home at least as far back as Jan. 2004!

The following is a brief rundown on what Tami S K and her gang of people, her posse as she calls them, have done since early 2008:

Tami, Plaintiff, has exhibited that she has no intention of following the law. And, according to the Supreme Court case lookup record also uses: Tammi, Tammy, Tami H, Tami T, Tami S K and just plain Tami K without the S, plus Tami Sue.

Tami, Plaintiff, according to the occupants of the home in the Injunction Against Harassment, J-1102-CV-200802799, threatened them with blowing heads off, when she arrived at their home on the 6th of December with several other people for no legal reason whatsoever, trying to throw them out of the house, which this Injunction was granted with a stern warning to Tami S K by His Honor Judge Bain of the Casa Grande Justice Court.

Tami, Plaintiff, has on numerous occasions attempted to take the law into her own hands by bringing a gang of people with her to forcefully take the home which in doing so not only placed the lives of her gang of people in jeopardy but also placed the lives of innocent people and Sheriff's Officers in jeopardy as the Sheriff's Officers arrived with guns drawn as evidenced by documents filed

by Tami, Plaintiff, with Judge Carter Olson and in Sheriff's Officers reports in which she was complaining about the Sheriff's actions to Judge Olson and by several police reports:

08002046	**080516134**	**080515073**	**080524130**
080524080	**080514124**	**081019115**	**080929110**
08009706	**081206056**		

Order of Protection J-1102-CV-200802203 against Tami by M Turney and Monica and since this order was issued she has violated it numerous times.

Injunction against Harassment J-1102-CV-200802799 Including threats of great bodily harm where His Honor Judge Bain sternly warned Tami that he would have her arrested and she would stay in jail for a long, long time, without bond, if he has evidence that she violated the Court Order.

The Defendant, the family in the home and Monica asks the court to not place their lives and innocent people with them in danger by ordering this violent person, Tami S K, the Plaintiff, and her gang, to actually fulfill her threats of killing them by allowing her to live next door to them.

Also please consider Defendant bought at the demand of the Plaintiff a one (1) ton dually truck from L G B that was given to Tami by M Turney and Monica as additional payment for her

extortion which cost $8,500.00 and a situation surrounding that vehicle which was given to Plaintiff at the same time as the $7,000.00 check which the Court did not address in its Notice/Order dated 12/5/2008.

More regarding the truck: Defendant and Monica were called recently by a Sergeant Ellsworth, I believe from the Sheriff's Office, about the truck because our telephone number was somehow on the record as the contact number for Tami, Plaintiff, and he stated that the one ton dually was impounded towing a trailer which contained a burned out vehicle that had been used in a HOMICIDE in Phoenix and they were trying to contact Tami and we informed him that she didn't reside at our home and that this was our phone number.

We might also point out that the 1996 Chevrolet Pickup 3500, one ton dually, with VIN Number 1GC xxxx **845 that Defendant bought from L G B is the same vehicle and that Defendant went to the DMV in Casa Grande Arizona on December 15, 2008 in an attempt to get documents showing the transfer of ownership in the truck to Tami and DMV would not release the information because the owner of record is Tami and to release it is against department policies but I am certain the Court could acquire the documents from the DMV if it so desired.**

There was testimony in Judge Olson's court by Tami xxxx, **her witnesses Patricia Be** xxxx , **Richard Ha** xxxx **and Fabian Or** xxxx **to which they admitted while testifying that they were involved in drug running, money laundering, conspiracy to commit those acts and using the house to run drugs out of which subjected Defendant and Citi Mortgage to seizure from drug enforcement agencies and what with all the criminal activity occurring at the home such as firing Ak47's, pistols and other activities of a violent nature, all of which were subjecting Defendant, Monica, their two children, neighbors and others to harm or death, which are all a proven matter and court record in the Casa Grande Justice Court during Order of Protection and Injunction Against Harassment trials.**

The Defendant asks the Court to consider the following document filed by the Plaintiff in this Court and the evidence submitted along with the testimony of the witnesses for the Plaintiff which prove many false statements.

In the Motion filed by the Plaintiff on CV200801499 date stamped by the Clerk on 08 Aug 11 AM 11:41 the Plaintiff repeatedly lied as proven in the trial held on December 3, 2008 before this Court. In review of this filed document:

The Defendant and the Plaintiff never "had an on going battle over this property for quite sometime" as she stated.

Evidence and testimony in the Court proved the Plaintiff never had any claim to the property in January 2004 or during the time that she claims they lived together as husband and wife. The Defendant allowed her to live there in a bedroom proving they did not live as "husband and wife" as she states and that her claim was all in her drug induced imagination and that she, Annette and her two children stayed in "her room". Evidence proves that she claimed the home belonged to her as early as January 2004 and that she Extorted Defendant into an Agreement later in 2004.

She also says "we were trying to leave the home (Annette, her daughter Maria and I)"….. This incident took place during the week and the next day was a school day for Maria and the school bus picked her up very early at the corner of xxxx **Road and** xxxx **Road. What kind of a parent would be leaving the home at 23:30 hours which is the time stated on the Sheriffs' Report dated 01-11-04.**

Evidence submitted proves they were drugged up, high on meth, lights on, music playing, talking loud and beating the child and telling her to "go to sleep" behind the dead bolted bedroom door and the Defendant yelled through the door and asked "how can she go to sleep while you are hitting her?" and that if they didn't stop he was going to call Child Protective Services on them and they stormed out telling Defendant that he was going to jail. The filed document proves there was a disagreement on January

11, 2004 and that it was over their abuse of the child.

Annette New xxxx **was a drug abuser and one of her friends at the time was trying to take her kids away from her because of the drug use by Annette. Her sister Rana Ama** xxxx **would not let Annette stay with her because the Sheriff was always stopping her car and searching it because of the involvement with drugs. The Plaintiff moved Annette into the Defendants house without his permission and wouldn't let the Defendant make her move and they dead bolted the bedroom door so they could do drugs behind his back while the kids were in the room.**

Evidence submitted proves she was still lying when she says that she got hurt, the police arrived, and the ambulance arrived and took her to the hospital. Prima Facia evidence proves she hit him with a "stick" as the officer says and she says they were in a "pushing match" and she admitted hitting the Defendant with a "stick". Obviously she lied in the document filed and didn't mention her knocking Defendant out and beat him with a rake and didn't get charged with Assault With A Deadly Weapon, she wasn't born with the rake attached to her body and evidence submitted proves she didn't hit him with a little "stick", she beat him with the rake as she admitted she did.

The Plaintiff in the document did admit, in the second paragraph of the document, that the County Attorney wanted to

prosecute the Defendant confirming that she told the Defendant, "it's a good thing that you took the plea bargain like I did because the County Attorney said he was going to have your ass and prosecute you to the fullest" and at the least, indicated that the County Attorney could have made that statement and that she, the Plaintiff, did in fact tell the Defendant that the conversation between her and the County Attorney did occur, but who can believe anything the Plaintiff says when evidence proves that so much of it lies.

And, in the same paragraph proved that she claimed she owned the home as early as January 2004, by saying that she got a restraining order against the Defendant which allowed the Plaintiff to take possession of his home, business, files, names, addresses, computers and everything he had and used them to EXTORT the Defendant into the Agreement she say, in the next paragraph, she got on April 24, 2004.

She continues in this filed document to lie by saying that she gave the Defendant 14,000.00 on March 3rd, 2005 and $5,000.00 on March 3rd, 2005 and $760.00 on March 5th, 2005 and $30,000.00 on March 23rd, 2005. There was no evidence to the claimed 14,000.00 whatsoever. And, she testified in Court that the checks she claimed to have given the Defendant that were signed by the deceased Tim K xxxx **years after his death on non-existent checking accounts were never cashed and prudently thinking, why would Defendant**

take checks signed by a dead person for any type of security? He wouldn't! One of the checks was on her personal, non-existent, checking account and it was signed by Tim K xxxx **years after his death. The Defendant did not take or hold these checks! And, the filed document claims a $30,000.00 payment which evidence, the receipt, proves was only for $20,000.00.**

The Plaintiff, in this filed document included a Certificate of Death showing Tim K xxxx **died on March 23, 2001, confirming that she forged the checks that she claimed to have given to the Defendant including her personal check dated in 2005.**

The testimony by the Plaintiff and all of her witnesses, prove that they were involved in drugs, which she admitted in this filed document, saying on November 2004, "I was arrested in KY" And, on May 10th, 2005 "I was re arrested for pretrial violation". The re arrest was for failing the prohibition against using drugs! They are drug users as well as drug dealers! Proving that the Defendant just felt sorry for her and tried many times to help her clean herself up and get off of the drugs.

And, in this filed document goes on later to complain about the police showing up and they, the Plaintiff and her posse as she calls them, were "at gun point" proving that she criminally takes the law into her own hands and did not pursue any purported claim in the Courts as the law requires of everyone and in doing so placed the lives of Sheriff Officers and many people in danger.

Then, this filed document shows that she tried to avoid any obligation to the Defendant by filing "July 9th filed chapter 13

bankruptcy" which was later dismissed by the Bankruptcy Court for her failure to file proper documents.

All of the lies in just this one document filed with the Court prove she will lie and if she will lie in one document she will lie in all of the documents and to the Court.

This filed document proves and the testimony on the stand by the Plaintiff and all of her witnesses prove, beyond a doubt that she used the house for unlawful and criminal activity subjecting the Defendant to seizure by the DEA and the Defendant has a right to protect his and Citi Mortgages' interest in the property by evicting admitted unlawful and criminal activity.

This filed document proves that she was in prison, that the Defendant served notice to do repairs and take care of their animals as proven by the dead dog on the chain without food and water and to stop using the property for unlawful purposes on, according to the Plaintiff, "my fiancé", who was Fabian Or xxxx **and testimony by her witnesses prove they voluntarily vacated the property instead of doing the repairs. It proves that she gave authority over any claim, rental agreement, or, other claims to her fiancé Fabian O** xxxx **and when he vacated the property he did so with her approval and authority to do so as if he were her and acted in her behalf.**

IN CONCLUSION

Superior Claim 1 – THE DEFENDANT asks the Court to recognize the Superior Claim by Citi Mortgage, the Deed of Trust, and the fact that the Court would be <u>ordering the Defendant to Violate the Terms of the Deed of Trust</u> if the Court were to order the Defendant to give the property to Plaintiff;

Superior Claim 2 – THE DEFENDANT asks the Court to recognize the Superior Claim by the xxxx **family which was entered into prior to any claim by the Plaintiff;**

Superior Claim 3 – THE DEFENDANT asks the Court to recognize the fact that the Defendant only entered into the Agreement with the Plaintiff because the Plaintiff did set out purposefully by EXTORTION to take Defendants home; and

THE DEFENDANT asks the Court to address the payment by the Defendant of the $7,000.00 check that she acknowledged receiving which the Court did not address in its' Notice/Order dated 12/05/08 and to apply the $7,000.00 to the purported payments made for the last several months of 2005 and all of 2006 which is what the Plaintiff agreed to apply the money to which was a refund of the payments which she admitted receiving and cashing. And, to consider the $8,500.00 truck that she received as additional refund toward any payments made; and

THE DEFENDANT asks the Court to recognize the ENTIRE Agreement between the parties and the Court should recognize

that there is more than one term in any agreement and that the only term of the Agreement that was addressed by the Court was the term regarding payments. There were actually 17 (seventeen) TERMS to the Agreement including #8: keep it insured; keep it free of damages; #9: attempt to refinance; if the plaintiff should become more than 30 days late this agreement shall become null and void; Plaintiff may be evicted; #10: time is of the essence; #16: not store vehicles, scrap on the land, NOT USE THE LAND IN ANY UNLAWFUL MANNER; and more. The Plaintiff actually violated all of the terms and would like all of these addressed by a Court or Jury, however, THE PLAINTIFF AND ALL OF HER WITNESSES ADMITTED USING THE LAND IN AN UNLAWFUL MANNER, UNDER OATH, IN THIS COURT.

The Court did not address the unlawful activity in its' Notice/Order dated 12/05/08 and asks the Court to do so; and

THE DEFENDANT asks the Court to recognize his right to protect his interest in the property and his obligation to protect the interest of Citi Mortgage; and

THE DEFENDANT asks the Court to consider: Would a jury want the criminal activity living right next door to them? Would Your Honor want all the criminal activity living right next door to him? And,

THE DEFENDANT asks the Court to review the document the Plaintiff filed with the Court on CV200801499 date stamped by the Clerk on 08 Aug 11 AM 11:41 wherein the Court may determine that the Plaintiff made many false and misleading statements and the document itself proves many lies were made by the Plaintiff.

There are many cases where Courts have held Officials, those in Authority and others accountable for not protecting those seeking and needing protection!

RIGHTS TO PROTECTION from abuse came from Failure to protect cases that sometimes ended in the death of the women and the death of men by women! I don't want my friends, Monica, the kids or I to die because of the Plaintiff and her gang.

EVEN THE SUPREME COURT OF ARIZONA recognizes the Elderly are being abused and taken advantage of! The Defendant is Elderly! He is sixty-five years old! And, the Defendant needs protection from the Plaintiff! The Plaintiff has extorted him, beat him unconscious and framed him as being the one who started it, put drugs in his coffee day after day, and tried to kill the Defendant and more.

MONICA, who was brought into this case/matter by threats from the Plaintiff, is very aware of the Failure to protect by those empowered to protect!

See the Order of Protection to protect her from the threats by the Plaintiff, J-1102-CV-200802203 as exhibit attached and see the next paragraphs.

Monica's' Grandfather, who was a Court Constable and retired GM worker and her Grandmother were both MURDERED in their early 60's when the Courts and those in authority FAILED TO PROTECT them after several complaints to those in authority!

Monica and her family took the case to the MEDIA, filed a lawsuit against those elected officials and the County/State and won! Their case caused the laws, Nationwide, to change as States recognized they had been empowered and were OBLIGED TO PROTECT INNOCENT PEOPLE! Exhibits not attached for privacy purposes but are available for the Court.

THE PLAINTIFF and her gang are a dangerous and violent group! Defendant is Elderly and Needs Protection! Monica Needs Protection! The xxxx **family, whom are both Elderly, Need Protection! The Community Needs Protection!**

THE DEFENDANT asks the Court to consider that the Plaintiff by EXTORTION forced the Defendant to enter into the Agreement dated in May 2004. The Plaintiff started out in the 1980's pursuing the Defendant, whom she thought was successful, and continues to

this day to take advantage of Defendant and by EXTORTION is trying to take everything the Defendant owns! The Plaintiff continues to manipulate the system, those in authority and officers and continues to attempt to extort the Defendant and will continue to do so if the Court allows it! In fact, if the Plaintiff was a man and violent he would have been locked up so deep in the system that she (he) would never see daylight again for all the violence.

THE DEFENDANT asks the Court to consider the fact that IF THE COURT allows Tami xxxx, **Plaintiff, and her gang of people to live right next door to the Defendant, all of us who are trying to stay away from the Plaintiff out of fear, the Court will be subjecting Defendant or other innocent people to being killed by the Plaintiff and her gang of people!**

THE DEFENDANT asks the Court to recognize the Superior Claims and not allow this insanity, extortion, death threats and abuse to continue!

THE DEFENDANT would also like to ask the Court a question. The Court issued the Order to the Defendant dated September 8, 2008 and filed September 9, 2008 not to sell the property. Defendant consulted another attorney and the attorney said that it would be safe to say, arguably, that the Court had, three months before the trial, gave the appearance that the Court had determined the outcome of the trial and that the Court was going

to rule in favor of the Plaintiff, and in issuing the order froze the asset of the Defendant which he might need the proceeds from, for a proper defense, and he said, every Defendant is entitled to use their money and assets for defense purposes or for any purpose up until the outcome of any trial and even O J Simpson was able to use his assets for his defense attorney fees and other expenses during his trial.

THE DEFENDANT asks the Court to consider the fact that the Plaintiff, because of her trying to illegally and forcefully take possession of the house and not using the legal system, has caused the Defendant financial hardship by forcing him to stop his financial endeavors so that he could protect his interest, the interest of Citi Mortgage and the interest of Paul and Suzanne in the home and has paid thousands of dollars in attorney fees and other expenses and is not financially able to make the payments on the home, which will place it in foreclosure, without the income from the present occupants.

THE DEFENDANT asks the Court to consider, even if the Court determines that the Plaintiff has a claim to the home, that the determination does not mitigate the crimes and the endangering the Sheriff's Officers when they responded "with guns drawn" and other innocent people by the Plaintiff's criminal acts when she took the law into her own hands, several times, by not pursuing this matter in the Court, legally, from the beginning.

Instead of legally pursuing the matter the Plaintiff chose, as proven with prima facia evidence – the many police reports – to exhibit a criminal mentality by showing up with a gang of people, using force, threats of great bodily harm, threats of death and more, to forcefully take possession of the home.

THE DEFENDANT asks the Court to not condone or endorse such criminal actions by allowing the Plaintiff to prevail in the matter before the Court.

And, why did the Plaintiff wait two years after her release from Federal Prison? It wasn't because the home was occupied as she testified in the Court proceedings on December 3, 2008! A prudent person would realize that she could have started legal proceedings even if the home was occupied! The Defendants' theory, based on his knowledge of how the Plaintiff thinks, is the Plaintiff waited until she was informed by her gang, Richard H xxxx, **Kim G** xxxx **and others who live near the Defendant, that the Defendant had left town on a trip. They seized that opportunity to usurp the home, in Defendants' absence, which they thought would be without challenge, not knowing that the Defendant had already sold the home and property. They thought they would all be together again, have a free place to live and do or sell drugs and would force the Defendant to use the legal system to evict them which could take years.**

THE DEFENDANT would like to bring to the Courts' attention that the Plaintiff while under oath in the Justice Court in Casa Grande, during one of the trials granting Orders of Protection against the Plaintiff, stated, "I (Plaintiff) won't be staying in the house long" and she said, "Judge Olson Ordered me (Plaintiff) to immediately take possession of my house", but, His Honor Judge Bain, told her (Plaintiff) that she cannot threaten to kill people, which she will do, and gave her, after the third time in his Court, stern warnings.

THE DEFENDANT in trying to determine what she meant by "I won't be staying in the house long" has concluded that she knows that the home will go into foreclosure, she just wants revenge for some imaginary reason or wants to live for free even if it is for a short time and doesn't want the Defendant to have the home either. The Plaintiff may need psychiatric testing for an Obsessive Disorder or Fatal Attraction and the Defendant knows that he has a right to be afraid of the Plaintiff.

THE DEFENDANT doesn't mean to offend anyone by telling the truth and telling it the way he sees it. To the Defendant it's transparent that the Plaintiff is extorting him and trying to usurp the property and the many items of prima facia evidence speak for themselves and were not allowed to be presented in the Court trial.

The Defendant is 65 years old and just wishes that the Plaintiff would leave him alone, get a job for a change, stop living off of the system and living off of her victims and that he, the Defendant, could live in Shalom, peace.

And, in the interest of Justice, to prevent a miscarriage of Justice, the Defendant asks the Court to recognize the continuing Motion for a New Trial with a Jury and a new Judge in light of the new evidence presented to the Court or to rule in favor of the Defendant.

Dated: ______________________________

M. Turney

____

M. Turney, in Pro Per

xxxx **Road**

Xxxx, **Arizona** xxxx

Copies of this Notice mailed

This ______ day of ____________200___, to:

Tami xxxx

Xxxx **Boulevard**

Xxxx, **Arizona** xxxx

cc to: Vicky P. News

I would like to point out that from the day I fired the attorney and throughout entire process I have called the court or went to the courthouse regularly just to find out if the plaintiff filed anything or if the judge had ordered anything.

Another one of the issues I have with this judge is the clerks can't tell me anything a lot of the time because he has the file in his chambers and they can't get access to it.

That is a real problem! If she files something or he orders something and I don't know about it and have to file a reply or do something I've been ordered to do I would miss the date and could lose the case because he is hiding the file and because of court rules – "unjustice"!

Of course, the other problem is my life has been totally dedicated to the case: studying the law, the rules of the courts, the appeal rules and procedures and that's a whole new issue; to appeal his decision you have to file notice of the appeal with the same judge.

In any case it takes hundreds and hundreds of hours studying and typing and making certain the documents fit the rules of the court in their format such as heading, spacing, side space, top and bottom space, type size, paragraph format – you get the point.

On one call to the judges assistant I asked her how long does the plaintiff have to respond to the notice of superior claims and she said she thought it was ten days plus five days and five days for the mail but that I had to know the rules and follow them as if I was a lawyer.

That's really funny in light of the fact that the plaintiff didn't comply with many of the rules that apparently I have to follow. I wonder why that is?

So I studied some more and determined that the 23rd of January 2009 would be the right time to give her to deny the items in the notice of superior claims. She never did, by the way. Yet you will see the judge dismissed the superior claims in the hearing on February 13th 2009 and acknowledged that she didn't file a contest to anything in it.

According to the way I read the rules: the opposing party must file a response to any claim filed and properly served on them. She was properly served and she didn't file any contest to what was filed!

Chapter 16

The Rules of Court is like playing poker with a novice. They can tell you their one pair beats a straight.

Oh by the way: you're the novice.

On January 23, 2009 I filed a Motion for a Ruling on the Superior Claims which is one of those things that you have to do. If you don't file it then you are saying that there are not any superior claims.

By the Rules of Court she has to respond to it or she is saying that she doesn't disagree, or, she doesn't contest the superior claims.

M Turney
In Propria Personna

IN THE SUPERIOR COURT OF THE STATE OF ARIZONA

IN AND FOR THE COUNTY OF PINAL

TAMI S. K xxxx,	)	**No. CV200801499**
	)	
Plaintiff,	)	**Assigned to Hon.**
	)	**Robert Carter**
v.	)	**Olson**
	)	**Division 9**
M. TURNEY,	)	
Defendant.	)	**MOTION FOR**
	)	**RULING**
	)	**SUPERIOR**
	)	**CLAIMS**
	)	

Defendant, in pro per, moves the Court for an order recognizing the three Superior Claims on the ground and for the reason that there are no contested

issues of fact to be resolved herein, and that the defendant is entitled to judgment in his favor which was filed with the Court on Dec. 30, 2008 as "Notice Of Superior Claims".

This motion is based upon the files and proceedings and the Separate Statement of Facts prepared and filed herein.

Dated this __________ day of _________________, 2009.

M. Turney

____

M. Turney, in Pro Per

Post Office xxxx

Xxxx, **Arizona** xxxx

STATEMENT OF FACTS

On December 30, 2008 the defendant, in Propia Personna, filed with the Court a Notice of Superior Claims. The document consisted of forty-four pages of uncontested facts along with seventy-eight pages of supporting evidence consisting of exhibit A through exhibit X.

The Superior Claims consisted of: Superior Claim 1: Citi Mortgage;

Superior Claim 2: xxxx **Family; and,**

Superior Claim 3: The Defendant.

Superior Claim 1, Citi Mortgage, was, and remains, uncontested by the Plaintiff, the Defendant and the Court during trial held on December 3, 2008.

Superior Claim 2, the xxxx **Family, are entitled to the occupancy and use of the property in this matter which was uncontested by the Plaintiff.**

Superior Claim 3, the Defendant is and was at all times the rightful owner of the property in this matter and that the Plaintiff only gained possession of the property after conspiring to have the Defendant arrested, lying about ownership to Judge Goodman and gaining a restraining order against the Defendant and by doing so gained control of Defendants files, records, computers, customer base, home, furniture and property and with threats of destruction EXTORTED the Defendant into an Agreement.

And, that the plaintiff with malice aforethought drugged the defendant each morning and night; conspired with Annette Newxxxx **to get him arrested; beat him with a rake; lied to the Judge in January 2004 by claiming ownership of the home and gained a restraining order to keep the defendant off of his own property and used the defendants property to extort defendant; continues to extort defendant as exhibited by recent telephone recordings and lies to this Court; continues to threaten the defendant and others with him or around him;**

And, to further prove the Plaintiff is lying to the Court the Plaintiff stated, under oath, that the defendant was involved with her in their drug ring. However, as proven by the testimony of her

witnesses, the defendant was not involved with their drug ring and the plaintiff's witness, Fabian Orxxxx**, testified that the defendant was "aware of what WE were doing", which proves that was what they were doing and also proves that the Plaintiff, while under oath, was lying! The defendant was not and never was involved in their drug activity!**

Then the Plaintiff and all of the Plaintiff's witnesses, under oath, stated that they were using the property for drug running and money laundering which was a violation of the Agreement. This uncontested Notice of Superior Claims proves the Plaintiff violated many of the terms of the Agreement.

And that the Court did not address the credit for the admitted receipt of $7,000.00 by the Plaintiff as payment in full for the purported payments for the last quarter of 2005 and all of 2006 and in fact the Court has not addressed it at all in the Notice/Order dated December 5, 2008.

And that the trial Judge may have been biased against the Defendant as stated in documents filed by the Plaintiff with the Court and as the Plaintiff stated to the Defendant in early 2004.

All of these facts and the many other facts shown in the Notice of Superior Claims remain uncontested by the Plaintiff.

The uncontested facts prove Citi Mortgage is a Superior Claim, the xxxx **Family is a Superior Claim and The Defendant is a Superior Claim and that the Defendant is the rightful owner of the property in this matter and have always been the rightful owner. The plaintiff's claimed rights under the Agreement for Sale having**

been acquired by EXTORTION and lies! And, it would be a miscarriage of justice for the Court to rule in favor of the Plaintiff.

The Court should quash the Lis Pendens recorded by plaintiff and the defendant should be awarded judgment in his favor and defendant should recover his reasonable attorney's fees pursuant to A.R.S. s/s 12-341.01, and costs.

Dated this ________ day of ________________, 2009.

M. Turney

____

M. Turney, in Pro Per

Post xxxx

Xxxx, **Arizona** xxxx

Copies of this Motion for Ruling mailed

This ______ day of ____________200___, to:

Hon. Robert Carter Olson

Judge of the Superior Court

Post Office Box 946

Florence, Arizona 85232-0946

The judge also denied this in the hearing on February 13, 2009.

During all of this I was also working on the Counterclaim to sue her for theft of all the stuff in the house and damages to the house and the dead dog on a chain in the yard who starved or died of dehydration and I finally got it finished so on January 26, 2009 I filed it with the court. And he threw that out on February 13th also.

Chapter 17

The Law is only the Law when it works for the Law!

M Turney
In Propria Personna
Post Office xxxx
Xxxx, **Arizona** xxxx

IN THE SUPERIOR COURT OF THE STATE OF ARIZONA

IN AND FOR THE COUNTY OF PINAL

TAMI S. K xxxx,	)	**No. CV200801499**
	)	
Plaintiff,	)	**Assigned to Hon.**
	)	**Robert Carter**
v.	)	**Olson**
	)	**Division 9**
M. TURNEY,	)	
Defendant.	)	**COUNTERCLAIM**
	)	
	)	

Defendant, in pro per, herein files a counterclaim against the Plaintiff in this matter for extortion, damages and destruction of the property which is the subject in the matter before the Court and for theft of personal property from inside the residence with a priceless value as many of the items are irreplaceable and antiques having an intrinsic value far above their replacement costs as they were inherited and irreplaceable as described in the separate statement of facts herein.

Dated this _______ day of ____________ 200 ______.

M. Turney

M. Turney, in Pro Per
Xxxx **Road**
Xxxx, **Arizona** xxxx

STATEMENT OF FACTS

Claim 1: Damages and Destruction of Home and Property

The defendant will show evidence proving the plaintiff broke windows, doors, screens, destroyed the carpeting inside the home, damaged walls and ceilings, roofing blown off that remained unrepaired, Extorted the defendant, abandoned the property and other damages that are in fact far beyond normal wear and tear and all of which are in violation of the Agreement between the defendant and the plaintiff which is the subject of the matter before the Court; and

The defendant will show that the property was literally trashed with junk, old vehicles, a dead dog on a chain that perished because of lack of food and water, fences in disrepair, junk, trash and garbage piled in the yard and more; and

The defendant will show that the property was being used for unlawful purposes, specifically: money laundering, drug running and drug dealing and other criminal activity by the plaintiff and her friends; and

The defendant will show the destruction of defendant's property including computers, files, tax records, company records,

business papers and more which was piled in the rain on the porch by the plaintiff when the plaintiff in January 2004 made false statements to the officers and courts claiming ownership of the home and property and extorted defendant into an agreement; and

The defendant will show a conspiracy between the plaintiff and Annette New xxxx **and other friends of plaintiff to frame the defendant have him thrown in jail for something he didn't do, gain possession of and usurp his property.**

Claim 2: Theft of Personal Property

The defendant will show that friends of the plaintiff moved the items that belonged to the plaintiff into a mini storage unit which was relocated by Mobile Mini to the home of Richard xxxx, **one of plaintiff's friends, and while moving the items belonging to the plaintiff they moved many items that belonged to the defendant; and**

The defendant will show by numerous police reports and statements by the officers involved and by the plaintiff herself in documents filed with the Court that the plaintiff broke into the house and caused damages and expenses for replacement of the locks, windows and doors that were damaged during the break in; and

The defendant will show that the plaintiff took many items that were in the home prior to the break in that belonged to Monica while the plaintiff was removing items from the home that she had placed into the home after breaking in and that many of

those items were inherited from the deceased grandparents of Monica which are irreplaceable and that Monica would like those items returned to her in the good conditions they were when they were taken by the plaintiff.

Partial List of Items Taken by the Plaintiff

Master bedroom set that the defendant had purchased from the deceased parents of the plaintiff;

Wrought Iron yard set that the defendant had purchased from the deceased parents of the plaintiff;

Two bedroom sets that the defendant had purchased at the time of purchasing the home from Stamey's Home Sales;

End tables and coffee table set belonging to Monica xxxx**;**

A priceless Antique Rug from India that was an heirloom which belonged to Monica xxxx**;**

Five wall paintings belonging to Monica xxxx **that were inherited from the estate of her deceased grandparents;**

Two brass end table lamps that belonged to Monica xxxx**;**

Dishes, a setting for 12, with 24kt gold trim belonging to Monica xxxx**;**

Three 19" color remote controlled television sets belonging to Monica xxxx**;**

Porcelain Doll that the dress opened into an umbrella that belonged to Monica xxxx**;**

Antique Wooden Hat Box from the 1800's that contained an 1800's style hat that belonged to the deceased great-grandmother

of Monica xxxx **which she inherited;**

Antique Glass Bottles from the early 1800's that Monica xxxx **had inherited from her grandmother;**

And, more items yet to be determined.

In Summation

The plaintiff in fact extorted the defendant into an agreement that the defendant would not have entered into under normal circumstances;

The plaintiff in fact did or allowed her boy friend and friends to do thousands of dollars in damages to the home which remained unrepaired when she abandoned the home;

The plaintiff in fact did or allowed her friends to remove many items that belonged to the defendant when they, as testified in the Court on December 3, 2008, moved everything from the home for the plaintiff;

The plaintiff in fact, when the plaintiff and her friends broke into the home, brought items into the home and later moved out the items plaintiff had brought in along with many items that belonged to Monica xxxx **which will be proven by statements made by Police Officers and other witnesses.**

Relief Sought

The defendant moves the Court to accept the delay in filing the counterclaim due to investigation, counsel and newly

discovered photographs, documents, recorded messages and evidence; some was presented during the trial by the plaintiff and plaintiff's witnesses in this Court on December 3, 2008. In addition;

The defendant moves the Court to find the plaintiff extorted the defendant into an agreement and subsequently violated many terms of that agreement and that the defendant acted properly in demanding plaintiff do repairs needed and after plaintiff abandoned the property acted property in evicting plaintiff for violation of the extorted agreement as per the terms of the agreement; and

The defendant moves the Court to order plaintiff to pay the costs of all damages to the home and for all costs to remove the junk from the yard which were all a violation of the Agreement between the defendant and plaintiff; and

The defendant and Monica move the Court to order the plaintiff to return all items taken from the home in as good a condition as when they were removed from the home by the plaintiff as the items are irreplaceable and priceless.

Or, in the alternative, to order the plaintiff to pay at least $100,000.00 in damage cost including the loss of the priceless items belonging to Monica.

And, the defendant moves the Court to quash the Notice of Lis Pendens filed by the plaintiff.

And, to award defendant any other damages the Court deems appropriate.

Dated this _______ day of __________________ 200 ______.

M. Turney

____

M. Turney, in Pro Per

Post Office xxxx

Xxxx, **Arizona** xxxx

Copies of this Counterclaim mailed

This ______ day of ____________200___, to:

Hon. Robert Carter Olson

Judge of the Superior Court

Post Office Box 946

Florence, Arizona 85232-0946

Tami S. K xxxx

Xxxx **Boulevard**

Xxxx, **Arizona** xxxx

As you can see she did a lot of damage to the house and took a lot of valuable items that didn't belong to her.

Then one day in late January I was in the electric company office and decided I wanted the electrical use record for the home and asked them to look that up for me. They found that while she was living in the home that someone there changed the electricity to my name and since I have several electric bills for different accounts I actually paid their electric use for about a year. They stole my identity and got it changed to my name!

So I filed a motion to amend the payment record with the court. It was denied on February 13th also.

Chapter 18

Asking for Justice is like playing the lottery! Justice and Injustices are drawn from the lottery pool at random - if you are not one of the affluent or well educated or a friend of the judge

M Turney

In Propria Personna

Post Office xxxx

Xxxx, **Arizona** xxxx

IN THE SUPERIOR COURT OF THE STATE OF ARIZONA

IN AND FOR THE COUNTY OF PINAL

TAMI S. K xxxx, **Plaintiff,**	)	**No. CV200801499**
v.	)	**Assigned to Hon. Robert Carter Olson Division 9**
M. TURNEY, Defendant.	)	**MOTION TO AMEND PAYMENT RECORD FILED WITH THE COURT**

Defendant, in pro per, moves the Court to allow the defendant to modify the payment record submitted to the Court based on newly discovered evidence acquired from Arizona Public Service, herein APS, concerning the amount of money owed to the defendant by the plaintiff.

This motion is based upon the files and proceedings and the Separate Statement of Facts prepared and filed herein.

Dated this __________ day of __________________, 2009.

M. Turney

____

Xxxx **M. Turney, in Pro Per**

Xxxx

Xxxx

STATEMENT OF FACTS

The Defendant will show that on December 10, 2004 the utilities, including APS for the electricity provided to the home at xxxx, **was changed to the name of Mac Turney, defendant, which he paid and while the plaintiffs' boyfriend and many other people, lived in the home up until January 3, 2006 totaling $2,175.03 and water bills of $480.00 for a total of $2,655.03 that should be deducted from any Court ordered credit, if any, to the plaintiff and credited as owed by the plaintiff to the defendant.**

In addition, the Statement filed with the Court stated on page two that the plaintiff was given a check for $7,000.00 which plaintiff admitted cashing and a truck that cost $8,500.00 however these amounts failed to carry over to the "Amount" column as a balance owed by the plaintiff to the defendant (or a credit if appropriate).

The defendant will show that by giving the defendant the appropriate credit for utilities, credit for the check for $7,000.00

and the truck that the balance owed to defendant by the plaintiff is $19,675.03.

RELIEF SOUGHT

The defendant moves the Court to grant modification of the Statement filed with the Court to properly apply the $7,000.00 paid to the plaintiff by the defendant.

The defendant moves the Court to grant modification of the Statement filed with the Court to properly apply the $8,500.00 paid to the plaintiff by the defendant.

The defendant moves the Court to grant modification of the Statement filed with the Court based on newly acquired evidence that the defendant paid the utilities for over a year which amounted to $2,655.03 which the plaintiff owes to the defendant and which should be deducted for any credit that the Court is considering granting to the plaintiff.

The defendant moves the Court to grant a Total Credit to the defendant in the amount of $19,675.03 which would place plaintiff delinquent from mid 2005.

The Court should quash the Lis Pendens recorded by plaintiff and the defendant should be awarded judgment in his favor and defendant should recover his reasonable attorney's fees pursuant to A.R.S. s/s 12-341.01, and costs.

Dated this ________ day of ________________, 2009.

M. Turney

____

M. Turney, in Pro Per

Xxxx

Xxxx

Copies of this Motion mailed

This ______ day of ____________200___, to:

Hon. Robert Carter Olson

Judge of the Superior Court

Post Office Box 946

Florence, Arizona 85232-0946

Tami S. xxxx

Xxxx

Chapter 19

"In general, the art of government consists of taking as much money as possible from one party of the citizens to give to the other. .... Voltaire (1764)"

There were so many things that that I didn't put in the court documents because I didn't remember them during the rush to complete and get them filed and the lawyer didn't use any of it for trial.

When she followed me from Cottonwood to Phoenix she stayed

at a house where some friends lived, Ron and Camille and their daughter Deedee who was only fifteen. They, including Deedee, were all alcoholics and smoked pot, and Deedee's' boyfriend who shared her bedroom was twenty-five years old. He's the one that I caught in the bed with Tami and Deedee where we lived that morning.

In any case, within a few days, I came home from work and Deedee and Tami were at home drinking, and now that I know about the drugs, probably doing cocaine and they were in nighties, flimsy night gowns. Apparently Deedee was spending the night.

It was about 9:00 PM when I got there and one of them handed me a beer. After a couple beers, while Tami and I were sitting next to each other on one of the couches Deedee sat down on my lap and was wriggling around sexually.

As I was standing up I was picking her up by her waist with both hands and I said, "we're not going there Deedee!" I was looking at Tami while I was saying it.

Apparently they were trying to set me up with an underage girl so they could control me or have me arrested or something. They decided to go to her moms' house so they got dressed and left. I went to bed as I had work the next day.

Another thing that occurred during this time span was one evening when I came home from work she wanted the two of us to go visit a girlfriend of hers and I said that I was tired and wanted to just relax and stay home, and that I had to go to work early the next day.

She kept insisting and ended up saying that she was going and I said that I wanted to spend some time with her and that I didn't want her to go. It's obvious now that her need for cocaine was more powerful than logic.

She got angry and threw something at me. Then her anger got out of control and she started busting up my furniture and anything she could grab. I pushed her up against the wall with my open hands on her chest and held her there and told her to stop busting up my stuff!

She appeared to calm down and I let her loose and we talked calmly for a minute.

When I turned and walked over to survey the damage she went out the front door and down the sidewalk to a neighbors house and apparently called the police.

When they pulled up out front I went to the door and they asked for her so I told them where she was and pointed that direction.

The two of them went to the neighbors and all three of them came back to the house where I met them at the opened door. When we walked in the living room and they saw the damage one of them grabbed me and was going to handcuff me.

I said, "I didn't do this, she did!" He looked at her. I said, "Tell him." She said, "Yeah, I did it." He hesitantly let me go. They talked with us for a while and finally told her that she needed to go to a friend's house for the night and calm down and that they would give her a ride.

Wow! If it was me that broke the furniture, I was going to jail! But since it was her, she just needs to go to a friend's house and calm down! Unbelievable!

She went with them but in about an hour and a half I got a call from her. They had dropped her off at a bar where she liked to hang out and she was sorry and would I come pick her up.

I can't believe I was so stupid or maybe it was the drugs she was putting in my coffee, but I did go pick her up and we came back home and I assume she put more drugs in my coffee because we stayed up all night and I still went to work.

She must have had her girlfriend bring drugs to her while she was at the bar!

Another thing occurred during the time when she filed for a divorce but didn't complete, after she went back to work at the nude peek show club so she could get drugs. By the way, she claimed that she was only dancing and not prostituting, but I know better now.

She came home one morning about 9:00 AM after being gone all night and of course was always trying to get me to snort some of her drugs anytime she was on them.

This particular morning she tried to get me to snort a line with her and I said ok just to see where she was going with this. I believed that I could handle one time and wouldn't do any more.

I don't recommend it to anyone. It is a big lie! All it does is ruin your life and make you sell and spend every dollar you can come up with to buy more. It lies to you and says you feel good but in reality a normal healthy person would feel that way anyway but it keeps demanding more and more just to make you feel normal.

But I did recognize the feeling. It was the same feeling I had when we first met and when we got married. I said that to her and she confessed that she was putting drugs in my coffee morning and night when we first met and up until I made her get off drugs the first time.

But now she thinks that I'm her buddy – I did a line with her so she can confide in me so she tells me about a plan she has.

Apparently she and some guy she knows have formulated a plan to make a lot of money.

She wanted me to divorce her so she could get married to this older man who was rich. She's positive she can get him to marry her!

In any case after they are married she wants to introduce him to me as one of her friends and show him my horses and get him to go horseback riding in the mountains nearby.

Then the plan was, John, I believe her buddy's' name was John, was going to wait in the mountains and when she and her husband was riding horses there they were going to shove him off one of the high cliff areas and kill him to get all his money.

I said you're both nuts! You'll never get away with it! The investigators have been through this kind of stuff hundreds of times and they will figure it out and convict you! You need to stop drugs Tami!

She said well even if they get evidence I can blame it all on John!

I said, quit it! You're the man's wife! You're the one who benefits from his death! They'll get you for sure!

I told her that if she didn't get off the drugs that I was done with her! "And, I said, I mean right now!"

Apparently, I guess, I convinced her to forget the idea.

Little did I know that I became the new plan!

Ok, let's look at a really brief but factual review of the drug abuse, fraud and extortion by this criminal, the plaintiff.

She was putting cocaine in my coffee morning and night to get me to marry her;

She got pregnant by another guy within a few weeks after we got married;

She tried to set me up with her underage girl friends' daughter Dee Dee;

She wanted cocaine so bad the evening I wanted her to stay home that she busted up the furniture and police took her to a bar;

She got an abortion;

I was told by her doctor that she was pregnant and when she got that way;

She confessed and wanted help with the drug problem; I tried to help her;

She started a divorce so she could get back to drugs and prostitution;

She got back on drugs and nude dancing and told me to get a divorce or she was going to get a divorce anyway and they had a plan for her to marry and kill some rich guy but I talked her out of it and got her off drugs again for awhile;

She started disappearing for several days at a time every few months and I divorced her when I caught her in the motel with her brother and another guy;

She wanted help and came crying to me and again so I tried to help her get off drugs;

She got back on drugs and moved to Texas;

She came crying back and wanted me to help again so I did;

She wanted the house where I was letting her live in a bedroom; I told her no;

She conspired to have me locked up for hitting her when in fact she was trying to beat me to death so she could steal the home and everything else;

I couldn't go back to my own home because she lied to the judge and got a restraining order to keep me off my property;

She forced me through extortion and fraud and threats of suing me for getting hurt, to give her a rent to own agreement;

She went to prison for several charges of money laundering and drug running;

She abandoned the house while in prison and destroyed it and stole my property;

She through threats forced me to give her a truck and $7,000.00 to get her to give up any possible claim to the house;

She and her brother threatened me with extortion again and she threatened to kill us if I didn't give her the house;

She and her gang of hoodlums tried to forcefully steal the house;

She claimed in court that she owned the house;

She threatened to sue me for my other property and my business both on the phone and in her own courtroom testimony if I didn't stop fighting her in court and let the court give her the house;

And, it continues.

Almost everything above has been given to the court but apparently it doesn't do any good if you have a bad attorney, miss complying with some unknown court rule or if the plaintiff has a judge in her control or on her side.

In any case I am fighting for justice and what is rightfully mine so I took the next step according to how I read the rules and the law, as best as I can in light of not having a degree in law.

Chapter 20

Judges are people too. The have the qualities of greed and prejudice just like many, many people do

On February 4, 2009 I filed an Application for Order and Judgment in my favor since the plaintiff did not contest any issues in prior motions and notices.

M Turney

In Propria Personna

Xxxx

Xxxx

IN THE SUPERIOR COURT OF THE STATE OF ARIZONA

IN AND FOR THE COUNTY OF PINAL

TAMI S. K,	)	**No. CV200801499**
Plaintiff,	)	**Assigned to Hon. Robert Carter Olson Division 9**
v.	)	
M. TURNEY,	)	
Defendant.	)	**APPLICATION FOR ORDER AND JUDGMENT**

Defendant, in pro per, moves the Court for an order recognizing the three Superior Claims on the ground and for the reason that there are <u>no contested issues of fact</u> to be resolved herein, and that the defendant is entitled to judgment in his favor AS A MATTER OF LAW.

This application is based upon the files and proceedings and the Separate Statement of Facts

prepared and filed herein.

Dated this _________ day of _______________, 2009.

M. Turney

____

Turney, in Pro Per

Xxxx

Xxxx

STATEMENT OF FACTS

On December 30, 2008 the defendant, in Propia Personna, filed with the Court a Notice of Superior Claims. The document consisted of forty-four pages of uncontested facts along with seventy-eight pages of supporting evidence consisting of exhibit A through exhibit X.

This "Application for Order and Judgment" consisted of an additional 20 pages of restating and arguments as to why I am entitled to Judgment in my favor but I am not going to put all of those pages in this book.

They are a repeat of all of the arguments that I have given to the Judge before and would be very repetitive to you. However, you should keep in mind that you would need to do this if you are fighting a case yourself.

Note: they are called arguments because you are arguing or disagreeing with the statements made by the opposing party for whatever the case is about.

Chapter 21

"I contend that for a nation to try to tax itself into prosperity is like a man standing in a bucket and trying to lift himself up by the handle. .... Winston Churchill"

I knew that the status review was coming up pretty soon and I have been told by the assistant to the judge that it is a telephonic review. I don't trust the court and even though every document I have filed with the court gives my phone number I felt I had better file something officially notifying the judge of my phone numbers.

On February 9, 2009 I filed a formal notice of Contact Phone Numbers. (I will not include the filing in the book – it's just my phone numbers.)

On February 13, 2009, the date for the status review, I made the following notes in my documents concerning the matter:

When I received the Order issued by the court on Dec. 5, 2008 and after reading it I called the assistant to the judge as advised in the order and she said that no one would be present, it is a telephonic (over the telephone) review, she said. I filed a Notice of Contact Phone Numbers on Feb. 9, 2009, even though all the documents I have filed include a telephone number on the top of the document because I didn't trust the judge or the court.

The telephonic review was scheduled for 10:00 AM on the 13th so I called the court assistant at 9:50 AM to make sure that someone was going to call me. They said it was a court room review! What? I was lied to! I asked if the plaintiff was there and they said yes. The person who answered the phone said let me take your number to the judge so the court can call you. I said, "I filed a notice on my phone numbers several days ago!" Wow, this is crazy!

There is no way that I can make it to that Court on time. It is at least 50 minutes away. That Judge is crazy and I have no rights.

The court called shortly after 10:00 AM and the review was started by the judge.

The judge named off everything I had filed one at a time and denied it. I could not believe it. Most of them he didn't state a reason for denying them but on one or two he said premature (meaning it was filed before I was supposed to file it), in other words, it was against the court rules. He didn't sound like he had read any of them, just named the names of the motion or notice or stay or application or whatever, so I tried to argue the case with him and he denied my arguments.

He was going to order me to give her my house when she said something about an eviction of the people in the house so he said he would look for the papers and make a ruling on Feb. 23, 2009.

I'm glad and thank God that she asked about the eviction otherwise he would have ordered me to give her the house on the 13th.

I received a typed transcript from the court a few days later. (With errors that are now in the record so as you will see in Chapter 24. I had to file a notice of error on February 23, 2009.)

The following is the order I received from the Judge.

10:07 a.m. hearing begins
11:00 a.m. hearing ends

IN THE SUPERIOR COURT

PINAL COUNTY, STATE OF ARIZONA

Filed In Court Record

Date Filed: 02/13/2009
Time Filed: 04:11 PM

DATE: 02/13/2009

THE HON ROBERT CARTER OLSON
Division: 9
Court Reporter: SAND. ___ MOR.: .

KRISTI YOUTSEY , CLERK
By, BARBIE D. ___ Deputy Clerk.

TAMI S ,
Plaintiff(s),
vs.
TURNEY,
Defendant(s).

CV200801499

MINUTE ENTRY ACTION:

STATUS REVIEW

PRESENT:

Plaintiff appearing in propria persona.

Defendant appearing telephonically in propria persona.

The Court announces this is the date and time set for Status Review.

THE RECORD MAY SHOW that Mr. Howard K has been withdrawn as counsel for defendant and all future minute entries shall be sent to the defendant directly.

The Court has reviewed the file and has read and reviewed the Motions filed.

As to the Motion to Withdraw Counsel which is also a Motion for New Trial.

Defendant presents statements to the Court as to said Motion.

The Court advises that everything that is in the Motion and statements made would seem to be information that the defendant had at the time of the trial and could have presented at the time of the trial.

Defendant advises that new evidence is contained in Notice of Superior Claims filed December 20, 2008.

The Court FINDS that there is no basis presented for which the Court can grant a new trial therefore;

102 CV200801499 Page 1 of 4

IT IS HEREBY ORDERED the Motion for a New Trial is denied and the Motion to Amend the Payment Record for similar reasons is denied.

The Court notes that there has been a Counterclaim filed and it was filed without prior authorization by the Court and was filed after the trial was completed, therefore the Counterclaim is improper and the Counterclaim is struck.

As to the Motion for Ruling on Superior Claims.

The Court FINDS there is nothing to rule on in respect to the issues raised in the Notice of Superior Claims. In the Courts prior ruling following the trial the Court only made the determination as to the Claim for Possession as between the defendant and the plaintiff. Other persons were not parties to the litigation and therefore the Court cannot determine the priority of those claims based on persons that were not parties to the litigation.

An Application for Order and Judgment which is a request to vacate the Court's prior Judgment and grant Judgment directly to the defendant and is filed in open court at this time; IT IS ORDERED denying this request.

A Request for Stay, which shall be filed in open court at this time, the Court FINDS that the prior Judgment was not a final Ruling for 54b purposes, therefore it is a moot issue as to Stay as it is not a Judgment that can yet be executed on. Therefore, the Application is denied.

The Court Finds that the defendant is making a further request for new trial.

The Court advises the defendant to review Rule 60 as to the standards for the Court setting aside a prior Judgment. The Court further advises the defendant the defendant's right to appeal has not yet attached as the Court has not yet issued a final ruling.

Discussion of Court and parties regarding the D . family that is living in the house.

Based on the Court's current Judgment it would be that the Plaintiff would continue making the payments as she had with the current loan balance of $78,800.00, plus having a judgment against Mr. Turney for the $14,560.00, plus interest dating back to the 2005 date indicated in the ruling. If the possession cannot be returned to the Plaintiff, the defendant will be looking at a judgment for what the lost value is of that property.

The Court advises that the current occupants of the house are not parties of this lawsuit.

Defendant presents further statements regarding agreements made by the plaintiff.

The Court has not made any determination as to anything involving the persons occupying the house.

Discussion of court and defendant regarding the agreements the defendant has made with other parties and the Court encourages the defendant to seek legal counsel.

Defendant presents statements and advises that he did not have an opportunity to object regarding a conflict with the Court proceeding on this case when he was County Attorney.

The Court FINDS that on September 8, 2008 the Court specifically addressed the issue of whether or not there was a conflict with the Court concerning some criminal charges that apparently occurred when the Court was County Attorney in 2004. The Court has no memory of any litigation involving the parties, the Court did raise the issue and there was no request that the Court recues himself and there was stipulation presented by the parties and on the record on October 10, 2008 that there was no conflict in this matter for the Court to proceed, therefore, the Court cannot set aside Judgment on that ground.

Discussion of Court and parties regarding a possible settlement.

The Defendant presents statements and advises that if he is ordered to make the payments he will not be able to make the payments and the property will go into foreclosure.

The Defendant presents an offer the Plaintiff that she make payments of $1,000.00 a month for 40 months for the equity in the house above the payment.

The Plaintiff is not willing to accept the offer from the Defendant.

The Court advises that the plaintiff is going to have to start making the payments once she gets back into the home and there is no reason why those payments cannot be forwarded on to CITI Mortgage.

Plaintiff presents statements regarding other property in Arizona and lawsuits pending.

The Court is going to reduce this judgment to a final order.

IT IS ORDERED directing that a certified copy of the order be forwarded to the plaintiff at no charge and that will bring this to a final matter where it will be subject to appeal.

Plaintiff advises that she has already filed a Forcible Detainer in Maricopa and that they were sending it this court to be handled. Maricopa/ Stanfield Justice Court CV 2008-1650 Tami vs. Suzanne and Paul

IT IS ORDERED this matter shall be taken under advisement for purposes of rendering a final judgment.

FURTHER ORDERED setting this matter for Internal Review only (NO PARTIES TO APPEAR) on February 23, 2009.

The Court will attempt to locate the forcible detainer that was sent from the Justice Court.

Plaintiff presents statements and advises that she needs to have immediate possession of the property.

Defendant presents further statements continuing to request for a new trial and continues objections to any ruling in the Plaintiff's favor.

The Court advises the defendant that he should review the Rules of Civil Procedure and review Rule 60 and advises that if he needs to file a Notice of Appeal in writing and is reminded that there is not a final order and it is not subject to appeal at this time.

Mailed/distributed copy: 2/17/2009
cc:
TAMI S K
PO BOX
CASA GRANDE AZ

M TURNEY
PO BOX
AZ

102 CV200801499 Page 4 of 4

In any case these few extra days gave me time to try to find something else in the law that was legal to file by the court rules.

I worked for over forty hours during the next three days so that I could file documents on Tuesday.

I had tape recorded the court review on the 13th on my recorder but it wasn't real clear and some words just didn't get recorded clearly but I was able to make out most of the things that were taped.

One thing stood out, he said something about I should be looking at court rule 60 to file motions under, I said it was rule 59 and he said no, it is 60.

I studied rule 60 and that rule pertains mainly to filing things after the final judgment. I wanted to stop him from making the final judgment because if he made it that would mean that I had to give her the house, now! Rule 60 don't work. He was in error! I was surprised that he even gave me any advice at all. Or, did he misguide me?

I then reread rule 59 and found laws that say it is appropriate to file before the judgment. Like I said, after many hours on this three day weekend I prepared another Motion for New Trial under Rule 59(a) 4: new evidence.

As you read on you will find that much of it is a repeat of what I filed under the Notice of Termination of Attorney and the Notice of Superior Claims which the judge denied on the 13th. You will also see that there are several changes, which are important, and make the document comply with Rule 59(a) 4. Rules of Court = "unjustice"! However, I will print all of the next motion because of changes. The areas that are repetitive must be done to comply with Court Rules.

Chapter 22

"I don't make jokes. I just watch the government and report the facts. .... Will Rogers"

M Turney

In Propria Personna

Post Office Xxxxx

Xxxxx, Arizona Xxxxx

Xxxxx

IN THE SUPERIOR COURT OF THE STATE OF ARIZONA

IN AND FOR THE COUNTY OF PINAL

TAMI S. K Xxxxx,	)	**No. CV200801499**
Plaintiff,	)	**Assigned to Hon. Robert Carter Olson Division 9**
v.	)	
M. TURNEY,	)	
Defendant.	)	**COVER SHEET FOR MOTION FOR NEW TRIAL**

Page	**Contents**
1	**Motion for New Trial**
1	**Point of Law**

Dated this __________ day of _________________, 2009.

Xxxxx M. Turney

____

M. Turney, in Pro Per

Post Office Xxxxx

Xxxxx

M Turney

In Propria Personna

Post Xxxxx

Xxxxx

IN THE SUPERIOR COURT OF THE STATE OF ARIZONA

IN AND FOR THE COUNTY OF PINAL

TAMI S. K Xxxxx,	)	**No. CV200801499**
	)	
Plaintiff,	)	**Assigned to Hon.**
	)	**Robert Carter**
v.	)	**Olson**
	)	**Division 9**
	)	
M. TURNEY,	)	**MOTION FOR**
	)	**NEW TRIAL**
Defendant.	)	
	)	

Defendant, in Pro Per, moves the court to grant a New Trial for the grounds listed below, which consist of mistakes and inadvertence, surprise, excusable neglect and newly discovered evidence which with due diligence could not have been discovered in time for trial as well as fraud and extortion by the plaintiff and other reasons justifying relief from the operation of the verdict and undue hardships on the defendant and the occupants of the home, the Xxxxx family, the subject of this matter and to consider the

following grounds in making the ruling for a new trial.

This Motion for New Trial is legal prior to entry of judgment. Point of Law: A motion for new trial which must be filed not later than 15 days after entry of judgment may be effectively filed prior to entry of judgment. *Farmers Ins. Co. of Arizona v. Vagnozzi (1982) 132 Ariz. 219, 644 P.2d 1305.* and/or:

A verdict having been reached in this matter as the Court has issued a Notice/Order in favor of the plaintiff. Point of Law: Motion for new trial and to set aside verdict and for judgment notwithstanding verdict was sufficient to extend time for perfecting appeal, though filed after verdict but prior to judgment. *Associates Finance Corp. v. Scott (App. 1966) 3 Ariz.App. 1, 411 P.2d 174.* and/or: Motion for new trial was properly filed after rendition of verdict but before entry of judgment, and, therefore, there was a proper motion upon which to predicate an appeal. *Dunahay v. Struzik (1964) 96 Ariz. 246, 393 P.2d 930.*

This Court has the authority to Order a New Trial. Point of Law: Under the Code 1939 provision authorizing court on its own initiative to order new trial at any time not later than 10 days after entry of judgment, read in connection with provision setting forth the grounds for new trial, a motion for new trial after verdict but before entry of judgment and order granting the new trial were not "premature" since the power to grant new trial may be exercised

by the court at any time after verdict, decision or judgment and for 10 days after judgment. ***Sadler v. Arizona Flour Mills Co. (1942) 58 Ariz. 486, 121 P.2d 412.***

GROUNDS

MISTAKE, INADVERTENCE, SURPRISE, EXCUSABLE NEGLECT

MISTAKE AND INADVERTENCE

The defendant was on vacation when the plaintiff started the matter before the Court and called the Attorney Referral Service in Arizona and was referred to Attorney Howard Xxxxx who they said had years of experience in real estate law.

The defendant retained attorney Xxxxx over the telephone and attorney Xxxxx filed an Appearance on behalf of the defendant but the defendant did not know that attorney Xxxxx was in his 80's and may in fact have medical or age issues that would prevent efficient representation.

And, the defendant wasn't aware that attorney Xxxxx may tire easily and not present a proper defense, counterclaim or be physically able to put forth the effort to properly counter the claim against the defendant.

SURPRISE

On the date of the trial the Defendant and Counsel went to a local restaurant and ate lunch and Defendant again asked Counsel to enter all of the evidence into the Court record and Counsel said no, that it was not needed. And, upon leaving the restaurant, Counsel became weak, grabbed hold of the exit door and almost collapsed and when Defendant asked if he was going to be alright stated he was weak and dizzy and to just give him a minute and he will be ok.

During the afternoon session of the trial Court, Counsel would sit with his head back, tired, sleepy, and dizzy and not object to anything presented by the Plaintiff other than saying early in the morning that he had "a continuing objection" to admitting the documents He wasn't representing the Defendant and upon closing argument did not offer any closing argument other than one regarding credit for caretaker fees.

In fact attorney Xxxxx was physically unable to properly put forth all the effort required to represent the defendant from the beginning of the proceedings.

Defendant on several occasions pointed out to Counsel that we needed to present to the Court all the evidence of violations by the Plaintiff in the agreement between the Plaintiff and the Defendant which is the subject of the aforementioned case number.

Counsel insisted that the Court would not allow the Plaintiff to enter into evidence any of the frivolous and unrelated information or documents she possessed and that the only issue the Court would consider is that he, Counsel, had filed an Election to forfeit and the Affidavit of Completion.

Defendant argued that since the Court was allowing three hours to hear the case that obviously there was a trial and that we should enter into evidence the documents and prepare by entering into evidence all items in the Defendant's possession to show the Plaintiff violated the agreement which, over Defendant's objections with Counsel both outside and inside the Court did not enter or present at the trial.

Counsel did not allow Defendant nor did he ever ask Defendant if Defendant objected to Judge Carter Olson presiding over the case.

In addition, attorney Xxxxx, did not enter into evidence that the subject property was, when the Plaintiff criminally tried to invade and seize possession of the home in early 2008 with a gang of her friends as evidenced by police reports, risking the lives of themselves and innocent people as police were called with guns drawn, under a sale agreement with the Xxxxx family after Plaintiff abandoned the property and multiple violations of the agreement by the Plaintiff and eviction as allowed under the terms

of the Agreement, who has spent several thousand dollars fixing up the property to their satisfaction so that they could live there for the rest of their lives who are medically impaired and retired.

Counsel did enter into evidence that page 10 item 18 of the Deed of Trust to CitiMortgage contains a Due On Sale clause which will place Defendant in violation of the Deed of Trust and accelerate the pay off which virtually places the property into Foreclosure for violation of the Deed of Trust and that the Defendant and the Plaintiff only intended the Agreement involved in this case to be a Rental Agreement wherein provided that if the Plaintiff paid the payments for approximately 30 years and did not violate any other terms of the Agreement that she would then be buying the home and that by the wording of the Agreement itself proves that it is and was only a rental agreement with terms and conditions that were all violated by the Plaintiff and that the Agreement itself was not formatted to be recorded with space above the heading and was not recorded until years later by the Plaintiff in an attempt to take the home from the Defendant.

Counsel did not allow Defendant to enter into evidence that Defendant recorded immediately after the Plaintiff recorded the four year old Agreement, a Notice of Violation of the Agreement in this case and a Notice of Termination of the Agreement for multiple violations of the Agreement by the Plaintiff as allowed in the terms of the Agreement.

Counsel did not allow Defendant to enter into evidence any of the following: that the Plaintiff was violating her agreement by using the property for dealing and transporting drugs and that she drove out of the driveway of the house involved in this Agreement in the vehicle that she was driving when arrested within a few days after leaving the home at Xxxxx Road and that the charges against her contained evidence that the vehicle seen driving out of the driveway contained drugs and/or cash; violated the agreement by allowing the property to be destroyed by both herself, her boyfriend and her friends; violated the agreement by not insuring it; violated the agreement by having her friends move her stuff out of the property and abandoning the home; violated the agreement by allowing it to be broken into repeatedly by people she knew who were using the house in its vacant state for drug dealing and drug use and leaving crack pipes and other drug paraphernalia laying around; violated the agreement by using it for unlawful purposes; violated the agreement by subjecting the property to seizure by drug enforcement agencies; violated the agreement in other instances in the agreement including "Time is of the essence".

Counsel for the Defendant did not allow the Defendant to enter into evidence with the Court the Defendant's Right to Protect His Interest since Defendant is obligated to CitiMortgage for the remaining Mortgage on the property and did not allow Defendant to enter into evidence the documents and photographs supporting

the badly deteriorated and damaged condition of the property and documents supporting the destruction of the property by the Plaintiff.

Filed with court on Dec. 11, 2008 defendant terminated attorney Xxxxx

Filed with court on Dec. 29, 2008 notice of change of address – in Pro Per

Filed with court on Dec. 30, 2008 notice of superior claims – in Pro Per

Filed with court on Jan. 30, 2009 attorney Xxxxx withdrawal from matter

EXCUSABLE NEGLECT

Counsel denied the Defendant the opportunity to present to the Court the intent of the Plaintiff to entirely bypass the Judicial System when she committed the following acts against the Defendant and the property involved in this case:

March 2008 Police Report 08002046
April 2008 Sheriff Officer Jordan Badge Xxxxx Phone Calls from Plaintiff left on his answering service threatening the Defendant
May 2008 Officers involved Reports 080516134, 080515073, 080524130, 080524080, 080514124

October 2008 Police and Sheriff Reports 081019115, 080929110, 08009706

December 6 2008 Sheriff Report 08011403 where Plaintiff and at least two other individuals in her vehicle came to the house and tried to throw out the occupants with threats and police advised the occupants to get an Order of Protection

December 8 2008 Police Report 081206056 where Plaintiff threatened Monica and the Defendant

Orders of Protection J-1102-CV-200802203 protecting the Defendant and Monica dated 09/29/2008 from the Plaintiff

Orders of Protection J-1102-CV-200802799 protecting the Occupants of the Home dated 12/08/2008 from the Plaintiff

Counsel denied the Defendant the opportunity to present to the Court the evidence supporting the Defendant's inability financially to support the Plaintiff forever and may in fact loose the home through foreclosure because of Defendant's lack of funds to continue payments on the house without the income from the present occupants.

Counsel denied the Defendant the opportunity to present to the Court the evidence showing that the Defendant was in fact protecting the house and that if the Court were to rule in favor of the Plaintiff that the Defendant should receive compensation from December 2005 of at least the amount of the monthly payments to CitiMortgage for custodial fees, for repairs and maintenance

required upon vacancy of the property where the windows were broken out, the roof was destroyed, the carpet was filthy from animals and stains, the yard was trashed, removal of a dead dog on a chain that starved to death without water and food and other destruction of the property which cost the defendant thousand of dollars.

Counsel for the defendant did not file a Counterclaim against the plaintiff for damages and costs; however, the defendant did file a Counterclaim with the Court on January 26, 2009.

And, defendant asks the Court to excuse his neglect in not stepping forward during the trial on December 3, 2008 and terminating the services of attorney Xxxxx when he should have been aware of the fact that he could have done so and for failing to do so when he was aware of attorney Xxxxx s' physical condition and fainting spell during the lunch hour and for failing to terminate the attorney/client relationship when defendant pointed out to attorney Xxxxx that all of the evidence should have been presented but attorney Xxxxx felt that only one item was important to be presented and that it was all that he had previously filed and that it would be improper to add additional evidence or documentation at this late date.

And, Attorney Howard Xxxxx will testify that he was not feeling well and suffered a dizzy spell during the lunch hour on the

date of the trial held on December 3, 2008 and did not efficiently represent the defendant.

And, attorney Xxxxx will testify that he did not present any of the evidence mentioned above that the defendant had asked him to present and that there are many items of newly discovered evidence that he was unaware of that would have most likely resulted in a different verdict.

NEWLY DISCOVERED EVIDENCE, FRAUD AND EXTORTION

The defendant has lived at his present address for 20 years and has a barn and storage building consisting of around 1,200 square feet. Over the years these buildings have become full of items the defendant has stored including many boxes of papers, business files, records, tax records, documents, computers and many other items and they are difficult to sort through to locate any particular item or items.

The defendant diligently worked many hours daily going through boxes and files in an attempt to locate pertinent items pertaining to the matter before the Court as well as typing, researching and filing hundreds of pages of documents and hundreds of pages of evidence with the Court and the new evidence

provided to the Court could not have been located prior to the trial.

And, in fact the defendant did not know if they existed any longer as the plaintiff had taken possession of the defendants property and files and records when she lied to Judge Goodman in January 2004 and the defendant had a restraining order on him to stay off of his property and the plaintiff did destroy a lot of the defendants files, records and photographs leaving the defendant in doubt that they still existed and of course some of the documents and photographs and other items belonging to the defendant were destroyed by the plaintiff and cannot be located.

Newly Discovered Evidence and evidence proving the destruction of the defendant's property, fraud and extortion attached.

And, recent new evidence that the plaintiff is still trying to Extort the defendant in the form of recorded telephone messages that were left by the plaintiff and her brother on the Qwest telephone recording service showing the date and time they left the messages and in their own words stating who they are, their phone numbers and that defendant better give plaintiff the house, recordings available.

And, defendant asks the court to reconsider the New Evidence and which with all due diligence could not have been presented at the trial as defendant didn't know the plaintiff had used his name to usurp electricity in his name that he paid for each month from APS and when asking for the usage record for Xxxxx Rd when he was at APS in late January 2009 the record showed the plaintiff had changed the electric to his name in December 2004 and defendant filed a Motion to Amend the Payment Record on February 3, 2009 and submitted evidence to the Court. This and other evidence in police reports prove the plaintiff is usurping the defendants identification and illegally using his name for APS, a dog in the city of Casa Grande by the name of Joker listed as at the address on McMurry where the plaintiff lives and defendant was called by the city and a police report was made with the Casa Grande Police Department and the plaintiff and her brother threatened the defendant with having social security number of defendant and other threats on tape, <u>exhibit Y.</u>

The Plaintiff recently filed Bankruptcy proceedings as evidenced by documents the plaintiff filed with the Court and testimony in Court and named the defendant as a debt for $17,600.00 and by listing the defendant and debt in the bankruptcy admitted owing the defendant and then the plaintiff called the defendant and left a message and threatening the defendant, <u>exhibit Y</u>.

Tami S K, the plaintiff, continues to this day to extort the defendant, <u>evidence in trial transcripts and in hearing on Feb. 13, 2009 transcripts</u>, ignore the law and violate and threaten anyone who gets in her way and to manipulate the courts for her own gain and she is assisted by many of the people she associates with. The Court should note the following damage to the property complaints, Orders of Protection and Injunctions against Harassment against the Plaintiff just since early 2008:

Injunction of Harassment, J-1102-CV-200802799 against Tami S K to stop threatening with death and harassing the Xxxxx family; <u>exhibit F</u>.

Order of Protection J-1102-CV-200802203 against Tami S K to stop threatening the Defendant M. Turney and Monica; <u>exhibit G</u>.

The Court should be aware of the Plaintiff's illegal activity against the property, the Defendant, Monica and the Xxxxx's as indicated by the City Of Casa Grande Police Reports and Pinal County Sheriff's Office Reports as follows: 08002046

080516134 080515073 080524130

080524080 080514124 081019115

080929110

08009706 081206056 plus others that are not be listed many of these are new evidence that could not have been

presented at the trial, exhibit BB.

In fact the defendant only entered into the Agreement with Plaintiff because of threats and Extortion and fraud.

The Defendant would offer to the Court the following brief story about how the Plaintiff gained possession of the property from the Defendant. None of this was allowed to be presented to the Court. This is a very short version but there were many more things that occurred because of Plaintiff's drug use:

Defendant met the Plaintiff when she was a hostess in Cottonwood Arizona and after she picked him up at the bar, after she ascertained in conversations and his use of an American Express card to pay the bill where she worked, and after spending the night in his hotel room and her girlfriend in the room of Defendants partner, that he was a successful business man, she soon pursued the Defendant by moving to Phoenix and near Defendants business where she said that she went to work as a hostess. Defendant was 46 and he found out later, she was 20 years old.

The Defendant worked 7 days a week in his business but was always full of energy and thought he was in love. Little did Defendant know that to get him, the Defendant, to marry her, the Plaintiff was putting cocaine in his coffee every morning and night

without his knowledge but Defendant thought he was in love, he was full of energy and within a month after meeting married her not knowing that the good feelings toward her were the drugs she was putting in his coffee. A few years later she confessed to putting cocaine in his coffee morning and night.

Within two weeks Defendant caught Plaintiff, a girl friend of hers who was only 15 and her 25 year old boyfriend in bed at the house the Defendant had rented but after denying that she had done anything, the Defendant didn't divorce her.

In a month the Defendant found out that Plaintiff was pregnant and had an abortion and the doctor told the Defendant that she had gotten pregnant in the first or second week of June which was when Defendant caught them in bed together.

Then Plaintiff confessed and informed the Defendant of her cocaine addiction and asked him to help her get off the drug(s) and confessed that she worked at a nude dance club, Pxxxxxx, for the money to support her drug addiction which she claimed she got from her bosses, Jim and Martin, at Xxxxxers.

After Defendant found out about her drug problem he told her to stop or that he would divorce her and she did stop for some time.

Within a short time she, the Plaintiff, filed for a divorce, so she could go back to work at Xxxxxers and get cocaine from her boss there, she said, exhibit K.

Defendant felt sorry for Plaintiff, told her to live her life the way she wants and she stopped the divorce. In time she grew tired of that lifestyle and asked the Defendant to again help her, so she could get off drugs, which Defendant did and then after a year or so she got back on cocaine and crystal meth and went back to work at Xxxxxers, a nude peek show club. During this time period she admitted to the Defendant that she was putting cocaine in his coffee when they first met.

Defendant couldn't take any more and divorced her in 1994 after catching her in a motel room with another man and her brother Jimmy K all together. This occurred one time, after many such times, when she had disappeared for several days but this time her horse was sick and dying in the pasture. I called one of her friends, Rana AmXxxxxas and told her about the horse and asked if she had seen Tami and she told me that she had saw Tami's car in front of Room 1 at the Xxxxx Truck Stop Motel on I-8. When I got there Tami's car was there so when I knocked on the door and stepped back to the window and when she opened the curtain to see who was at the door, she was naked, the guy was pulling up his pants and Jimmy, her brother, was still in the bed. So I filed and got the divorce, exhibit L

During the divorce she wanted the café and store that I owned and she agreed to pay me for the inventory if I would give the store to her. The place didn't make any money and I was happy to get rid of it, even though we had a pre-nuptial agreement, so I told her she would only have to pay me for the inventory. We pulled an inventory and she gave Defendant a note for $30,000.00, for the inventory.

Local people complained to Defendant that the Plaintiff and some of her friends were dealing drugs out of the cafe and in fact one of her cooks was killed in or near Superior Arizona around that time and according to the newspapers it was a drug related crime. His name was Garret or Garrett but I forget his last name.

In four to six months Plaintiff called the Defendant and said that Defendant could have the store and café back, because she couldn't pay the bills. Defendant drove to the store with a lady in his car by the name of Gail JozXxxxx and when we pulled up in the parking lot Tami, Plaintiff, came running out and threatened to kill Gail so we left and Gail had me drive her to the Casa Grande Justice Court and she took out an Order of Protection on Tami which was not contested by Tami, Plaintiff.

In a week or so Defendant received a final notice for an electric bill for over $6,000.00 from APS which was for the store and café, the account was still in his name, so he called her and

went to the store which was closed but Tami was there. She said you can have it back, threw the keys at him and drove away in her car. He went in and the inventory was totally gone, there was nothing left in the store or café to sell, just empty space, she had sold it all!

I paid the bills and re-stocked the store and café and in a couple days was driving by late in the evening and low and behold Tami, her mother Norma Xxxxx and father Tim Xxxxx and sister Sandra Xxxxx and two men were all coming out of my store with bags of groceries and the truck bed was full. I had neglected to change the locks! I ordered them off the property but they wouldn't leave so I called the Sheriff's Office. When an officer arrived I told him what happened but the Plaintiff lied and claimed she owned the store and café. The officer told all of us to leave and to take it up in civil court. The next morning Defendant changed the locks.

In 1995 or 1996 she came crying to me saying she lost her place to live and wanted to move into one of the rooms at my house. After saying no, several times, Defendant reluctantly told her not to move in very much because it will not work out and that she better not bring any drugs to his house. Her sister Sandra Xxxxx and her boyfriend Larry came by my house before Tami had moved anything into it. They were on their way back to live in Kingman. They sold me some videos and a bedroom set which I bought

because they needed the money to make the move and just before they left they told me, because they were mad at Tami at the time, these are her sister Sandra's words, not mine, "don't sleep with her, she has been fuxking every nigxer in Casa Grande, dealing drugs, prostituting and shooting drugs!" that is her words not mine

She stayed at defendants' house and would clean it sometime and cook at times and appeared to be off drugs. We didn't live as husband and wife! I wouldn't sleep with her because of my knowledge of what she was and her drug abuse.

At one time she asked me to write her a letter saying she got paid for working for me and I said that I would not do that. She was trying to buy a car or something and needed something to show income. I said well you are staying at my house free with free utilities that amounts to about a thousand dollars a month you don't have to pay out. She said to write something for $1,300.00 a month and as a second thought asked me to say it was a gift so she could get the car or for welfare or some other reason I am unaware of. Defendant complied with her wishes and she got a car but within a few months lost it because she couldn't make the payments.

The Plaintiff appeared to the Defendant to be off drugs and we were getting along fairly well for a while and occasionally we

would go to her mother and father's house in Kingman Arizona to visit for a day or two.

On one visit her mother and father were re-confirming their marriage vows in Laughlin Nevada and we were there and Tami, Plaintiff, tried to get me to re-marry her while we were there but I said, no Tami!

Another time we were at their house and her brother Jimmy and her sister Laurie and her sister Sandy all got into an argument and somehow I was drawn into it. Jimmy said he was going to kick my ass and said step outside. When we got outside he kept walking toward the entrance to the driveway instead of stopping in the clear area outside the door. There was a block fence at the entrance and when he got to it he turned to face me and was ready to fight but obviously wanted me to hit him first. I'm not big on fighting, I was a lot older than him and he was in better physical shape and out of the corner of my left eye I saw movement and there was their sister Laurie stooped down with a chrome pistol in her hand. I walked away and got in my car and Tami, the Plaintiff, jumped in as I was driving off and asked why I didn't hit him and I just said it wasn't worth it. They had it set up to kill me that time! Tami, the Plaintiff, denied any knowledge or involvement.

She kept pushing to re-marry and I said no every time! We didn't sleep together, I just felt sorry for her and tried to help her,

but in any case I wouldn't marry her!

In March 2002 I bought a manufactured home, the one she now is trying to claim is hers, from Stamey's manufactured home lot in Casa Grande and put it on property I owned, exhibit M.

Defendant let Plaintiff move into her own room and because he felt sorry for her and she seemed to still be clean of drugs he was willing to try to help her. Defendant was going to, later, rent out this manufactured home or sell it when the home he was building on the lot next door was completed.

In 2003 the Defendant had some money from selling a lot that he owned and a little more that he had put aside to finish the house next door so he went to work on it seven days a week and several times hired contractors for some of it.

One day when Defendant walked in he went directly to the kitchen sink to wash up and looked through the opening and saw one of Plaintiffs friends, Kim Xxxxx, trying to hide something from him in the couch. He asked, "What's that?" and she held it up, it was a crack/meth pipe and he told her to get out of my house and she said "It's ok with Tami" and I said, "it's not, get out!" Tami was in her bedroom at the time, I guess, as they had put a deadbolt on the bedroom door so no one could get in without a key which

allowed the drug use to go on in one of the Defendants bedroom, behind his back.

Then she let Annette Xxxxx and her two kids move in and when I found out I told them to leave but Tami, the Plaintiff, said that I can't make them leave and since I was near to finishing the house next door I didn't fight it even though I did tell her twice to take her kids and leave my house because of her being high.

By January 2004 I had the home almost completely built and Tami stated "when you move over there, I want this house!" meaning the manufactured home at Xxxxx Rd., to which, I responded, no! You can't make the payments! You don't even work! You're going to need to find another place to live because I am going to rent this one out to pay the bills or sell it if I can find a buyer who can come up with their own financing to pay it off! And, because of their drug problem.

On January 11, 2004 I came home from working on the house next door and they (Tami and Annette) were beating Annette's daughter in Tami's bedroom. I yelled at them to stop beating that girl and told all of them to get out of my house. They rushed out of the bedroom and Tami stuck her finger in my chest and said "you're going to jail"! "For what?" I asked. I said, "All of you get out!" Annette told her daughter to take the boy and go to the car. We all went to the front porch where I stopped just outside

the door, on the porch. Tami was in front of me and Annette and the kids were at their car. Annette was calling someone and said on the phone something along the lines of send the police, Mac is beating up Tami. I looked at her and all of a sudden things went black, Tami had knocked me out but I heard the glass of water that I was drinking hit the floor and I pushed her away. Apparently she jumped off the porch to the ground. Annette was saying hurry, I assume to the 911 operator and I looked toward her. I seen movement out of my left eye and instinctively stuck up my left hand. Something hit it HARD and it felt broken. I heard something slam down on the porch...whatever she hit me with had broken. I looked at my hand and grabbed it with my right hand, it hurt. Then I saw movement toward my head again...but I was too late...everything went black. The next thing I know is I was trying to lock the door from the inside of the house and the Plaintiff was pushing on it trying to get in. I got it locked and shortly thereafter the police showed up while I was in the bathroom looking at my head, face, hand, arms and legs...they were all cut and bruised. She apparently beat me unconscious with something and was trying to kill me, <u>victim copy of report</u>, <u>exhibit N</u>.

Needless to say...two women saying that I had hit Tami is a lost battle long before it gets started in any court in America. She said she was hurt and went off in an ambulance and I was taken to jail and I am certain the booking photo will show a lot of blood on me even though the officer gave me a wet towel to clean it off so he

could take the photo. She was charged also but got out, went to my home and managed to keep me out of my own home, <u>police officers statement</u> <u>exhibit O</u>.

The officer's statement confirms that the Defendant was the Victim. It confirms that Defendant was beaten with a "stick" according to the Plaintiff, but it confirms that the Defendant was hit with an object that the Plaintiff was not born with. It also says the Defendant was intoxicated.

The Defendant was not intoxicated, he was semi-conscious! If the officer took a test to determine the alcohol level of the Defendant he does not remember it but he is certain it would not show more than the level of 2 beers as he had drank 2 beers several hours earlier when he stopped work on the house next door. He was not intoxicated! He had just been knocked out once at the door by the Plaintiff! He was again knocked out and severely beaten with a rake by the Plaintiff. Plaintiff later admitted it was a rake! The Defendant was in shock and a state of semi-consciousness! The Plaintiff tried to beat him to death with the rake and even chased him into the house trying to finish the job. Plaintiff and Annette Xxxxx conspired to do great bodily harm to the Defendant and have him arrested for starting the fight as evidenced by threats in the hall before they went outside and by the phone call to 911 by Annette Xxxxx prior to the Plaintiff knocking the Defendant out the first time. Actually the beating by the Plaintiff was Assault with

a Deadly Weapon and if it were a man he would have been so charged, photos of Defendant taken a few days later, exhibit P.

The Plaintiff actually started in January 2004 trying to usurp the Defendants home when she told the police and obviously the Judge or someone in authority that she owned the home and the Judge upon release would not let the Defendant return to his own home, order from Judge Goodman upon release from jail, exhibit Q.

The next morning at around 9Am I went before a Judge Goodman, I assume, at the jail and he released me but said I could not go back to my house. I explained that I owned it and that I was letting the Plaintiff stay in a room in my house. He said that she said it was her house, and he asked if I was going to go back to the house and he stated that if I was going back there that he wasn't going to let me out! I accepted the terms and had a friend pick me up and stayed at his home in Scottsdale while I tried to figure out how to get those people out of my house and heal from the beating. I took the photographs within a couple days but some of the damage had healed by then. The Plaintiff had control of my office, my computers, files, papers and documents and everything I owned including my home! I was still in post traumatic stress. After a few weeks I moved into the home I had been working on next door even though it wasn't finished.

The Plaintiff had possession of everything Defendant owned including all of my business records, files and computers. She had the names and addresses of every business contact and all of their information. She had control of my life because someone ordered me not to go back to my own home; the home I had bought which was in my name only and Defendant wasn't married to anyone.

Defendant made arrangements with a court order for an officer to go with me to get some of my things but the officer said that she only had a few minutes so I needed to make it quick. I would end up with very few items and the officer and I had to go. The Plaintiff still had possession of 90% of my property and almost all of my business information, court order for police escort, exhibit R.

Defendant hired an attorney Pamela Xxxxx to help me deal with all of the false claims by the Plaintiff. We were working on this when the Plaintiff contacted me and said she had hit me with a rake and that "it's a good thing that you took the plea bargain like I did because the County Attorney said he was going to have your ass and prosecute you to the fullest." And, she tried to get me to feel sorry for her again and asked for the house and she said, if I would give it to her that I could have my stuff, but I didn't fall for it and I knew that Attorney Xxxxx would get my home and property back, receipt for payment to attorney Pam Xxxxx, exhibit S.

(Note: I did not include this statement in this court motion because it doesn't pertain to the case, however, it is interesting.

Pam Xxxxx specialized in Domestic Relationships between families.

When I retained her we discussed the situation and she asked me, "Does Tami do drugs?" My answer was "yes".

She replied that she had handled a lot of divorces in this area and that 90% of the women in the divorces were on drugs!)

(The motion continued:)

The plaintiff knew that she couldn't possibly convince anyone that she had any claim to the home and property: she was not the Defendants wife, she was just being allowed use of a room in the home of the Defendant while he was trying to help her stay off drugs but obviously she had started using drugs again and everyone she associated with were drug addicts and her name had never been on the title to the home. Plaintiff knew that she had to do something or she was going to loose her free place to stay; the Defendant had already told her she was going to need to find another place to live when he moved and she couldn't talk him into renting it to her – no job, no income, drugs and drug addict friends, etc., so she had to take it into her own hands somehow. Apparently she or they formulated a plan.

Then the Plaintiff contacted the Defendant again and began <u>EXTORTION</u> by saying that she had every name, address and phone numbers for Defendants business contacts and customers

and all of my records and my computer and files and tax records and that if the Defendant didn't give her the house at Xxxxx Road that she would contact all of them and would harass them to the point that they would stop using the Defendant for any of their work and that she would destroy everything of the Defendants, before he could get it all back. She also said that Mark Xxxxx, a neighbor, was a computer hacker and they had already sent out emails from my computer using my name and account and that they had messed with my computer, files and copied all of my information. And, that wasn't all they were going to do if Defendant didn't give her the house and property. To this day I do not know what they did with all my computer information and who they sent emails to or what they did to that computer and my files and customers.

So, in May 2004 the EXTORTION worked as Plaintiff, on top of the threats above, threatened to sue the Defendant for getting hurt when she, in her words, was pushed off the porch and was transported to the hospital and claimed her back was hurt on the defendant's property.

And, she pushed the EXTORTION harder because now she had piled all of the Defendants stuff on the back porch, in the rain, which would ruin all the files, records, computers, papers and books plus one of the couches and a chair so we entered into what the wording says is a Real Estate Offer and Purchase Agreement

which is the only way that she would accept it even though the Defendant tried to word it as a Rental Agreement with many terms and conditions that would prove that it is only a rental agreement and the Defendant figured that she couldn't live by it anyway because she didn't work, she didn't have any money and had no income, she had drug problems and more. That was the only way the Defendant could get back all of his personal property, business files and records and his computer and get them out of the rain and to stop her from contacting customers and totally ruining the business, <u>photos of stuff on the back porch in the rain, exhibit T.</u>

It was obvious to the Defendant that the Sheriff's Officers and County Attorney at the time and the Justice System was of no value in protecting him and that Tami S Xxxxx, Plaintiff, could get them to do anything for her and against the Defendant and they even allowed her to gain possession of everything he owned and ordered him to stay out of his own home.

Tami S Xxxxx, Plaintiff, had already proven that she could control the Defendants life with the manipulation of the Officers and the Justice System and had in fact gained full control of everything the Defendant owned since January 11, 2004 because of lies and getting a Judge to issue a restraining order against him by saying she owned the home even though her name was never on the home as an owner and they weren't married.

As further evidence that the Plaintiff by Extortion forced the Defendant to enter into the Agreement dated May 24, 2004 which is the matter before this Court, see exhibit U.

The Plaintiff was, at the same time that she had possession and control of the Defendants home, business, phones and everything he owned, after she beat him severely with a rake and conspired with Annette Xxxxx to frame him for starting the fight, threatened Defendant that she was going to file suit against him for getting hurt on his property.

When the Defendant agreed to sign an Agreement on the house, under duress by Extortion, the Plaintiff put some plastic over his stuff on the porch and she voluntarily gave the document to the Defendant stating that she "will not sue Mac Turney" which released another one of her Extortion threats that she was using to get the Defendant to do whatever she wanted. And, she allowed him to get his stuff that was on the back porch out of the rain but a lot of it had been destroyed.

The Plaintiff made a couple payments as shown in the Court and kept promising to pay what she owed. She said she had a good job that paid her cash to haul construction equipment all over the U. S. and that she should be able to keep up the rent payments. Her, her friends and a bunch of people I had never seen before

kept coming and going from my house for months with trucks, trailers, cars and assorted vehicles.

During the next several months she kept telling Defendant that she was getting paid for hauling construction equipment but they still owed her and will pay her soon and that she will pay the rent payments soon. Of course, Defendant was uncertain of what she could do with the threats, involved with his own life and let her slide for some time.

Some time in early 2005 she went to jail but at the time the Defendant did not know that it was for drug trafficking and that she was arrested in Kentucky. Her boyfriend Fabian Xxxxx kept telling Defendant that he would get the money to pay the rent payments because he had a construction job going and would get paid when it was done so again the Defendant let it slide for some more time.

When Plaintiff showed up at my house in mid 2005 with $20,000.00 toward payments, back charges and the balance of $10,000.00 to be decided by me once I was able to retrieve the payment history and to apply it as appropriate, I accepted it and gave her a receipt. Defendant knew it wasn't all that she owed and he gave instructions that she better keep the terms of the agreement in the future. He also suspected the money wasn't from hauling construction equipment and tried to contact someone at

DEA to report it but stopped out of concern over the threats.

Later the Defendant found out that she had been in jail for money laundering and drug related charges and that the vehicles they were arrested in (her, Patricia Xxxxx and several other people) were the same vehicles they were driving from his property (the house in this matter) because after she was released from jail in mid 2005 the same vehicles were coming and going and kept showed up again and later she told the Defendant that they were the same vehicles they were arrested in back in Kentucky but the DEA had given them back to her.

She went back to jail which Defendant understood was for a drug use violation. The home had been trashed but now it got worse, windows broken, roof torn off, junk in yard, old vehicles, dead dog on a chain tied to a tree and more, with people coming and going all night and day, photos of house damages, exhibit V.

Finally after seeing the trashed situation the Defendant went to her boyfriend Fabian Xxxxx and told him to clean up the place and do the repairs as needed and to start taking care of their animals or the Defendant would evict him as Tami, the Plaintiff is in violation of the agreement.

Not long after that he and all his friends packed up things and left. They didn't come back!

Shortly after that the Defendant was contacted by, I believe, Patricia Xxxxxez's daughter Anna, so they could get into the house and pack and store all of Tami's stuff in a Mobile Mini unit and move it to Richard HXxxxx's house because Tami was going to be in prison for three years, they said. So, I let them do that! Her own witnesses in the Court prove they moved her stuff and abandoned the home.

Afterward, the place was abandoned and falling apart. I posted a notice of violation on the house and evicted an empty house and used the notice to notify her friends who were still coming around, after they violated every term in the agreement and the home was falling apart. The house was getting broken into by her friends, even with the notice on the door and gate and they were leaving drug paraphernalia laying around and doing a lot of damage to the place. After we did extensive repairs to the place, new windows and doors, screens, cleaned the carpet twice to get out the stink from animals, cats, dogs, ferrets, birds and more, painted and fixed the rooms and removed all the junk from the yard which cost several thousand dollars we put our son and daughter in the house as caretakers and we paid the utilities to keep the place from getting destroyed and burned down by drug addicts which in doing so cost Defendant $760.00 a month for caretakers.

Defendant had some contact with the Plaintiff but at a distance because she had made threats to him and extorted the Defendant and he knew that she could use the court system to get what she wanted. He didn't know what she was capable of doing but it was obvious that the Plaintiff and Patricia Xxxxx could manipulate the Courts and end up only getting three years, when the men involved got 30 years to life, and they could have got the same sentence. It was already obvious that Plaintiff could manipulate officers and the courts in this area too and that the Defendant would be the one in trouble. Plaintiff even made a threat to kill the Defendant by saying "those guys will kill for me", while pointing toward Fabian Xxxxx and three or four other guys in the yard and that a certain friend of hers, Gums as he is known, would kill anyone for her if she just told him to.

No one ever made any payments to the mortgage company other than the Defendant! And, he continues to make the payments to Citi Mortgage to this day! The mortgage is in the Defendants name only and always has been.

Lo and Behold after all these years the Plaintiff decides to usurp the house after violating all the terms, abandoning it for years and not making the payments and recording a four year old document that the Plaintiff, <u>with malice</u> <u>by threats and extortion forced the Defendant to enter into</u> which was written as a Rental Agreement with clauses that allowed her to buy it if she paid the

payments for 30 years and didn't violate the other terms of the agreement such as trashing it, letting it fall apart, not making payments, not using it for illegal use, etc. Plaintiff violated many of the terms of the Agreement! PLUS, THE PLAINTIFF AND ALL OF HER WITNESSES ADMITTED ON THE WITNESS STAND IN THE COURT THAT THEY WERE USING THE HOME FOR UNLAWFUL ACTIVITY INCLUDING DRUG AND MONEY LAUNDERING!, which this Court ignored. Defendant thought any Court would recognize all the terms of an Agreement and that the Agreement which includes EVERY TERM within it would be upheld by any Court.

In return Defendant recorded the second eviction notice that was posted at the house in 2006 Fee Number: 2008-052071, just a few days after Plaintiff recorded the (4) four year old agreement that was null and void in his best judgment and gotten by Extortion.

Later, in 2007, to satisfy threats by Plaintiff, Defendant gave her a 1 ton dually he purchased for her for $8,500.00 and a check for $7,000.00 saying paid in full which she cashed (which is what she asked for) to terminate the 2004 Agreement, along with the hand written agreement that she made stating that this was payment in full for any claims she may have against the Defendant forever. Exhibit W + Z. (See more regarding the truck towing a car that was used in a Homicide.)

As criminal minded as the Plaintiff, Tami S Xxxxx is, the Defendant knew better and should have never trusted that she would honor any agreement!

In 2008 Tami, Plaintiff, started trying to forcefully steal the property from Defendant and with a gang of her hoodlum friends showed up, cut the lock and chain off of the gate, burglarized the house and changed all of the locks but Officers have managed to temporarily keep her at bay but the threats of harm are real if she isn't stopped.

When it turned out that the Plaintiff couldn't forcefully take the house she started the Extortion all over again only this time with different threats.

Plaintiff called the Defendant while he was on vacation and threatened that he had better give her the house or she would take his business, claim that he cheated on his taxes, tell the real estate board that he was selling real estate without a license and claim that he was involved or had knowledge of the Drug Activity that the Plaintiff, Patricia Xxxxx, Fabian Xxxxx (by his own testimony before this Court) and others were involved in. All of which are lies and the Defendant wouldn't give her the house so she, the Plaintiff, has followed through with these threats by calling the IRS, the real estate board and by the Plaintiff and all of her witnesses

committing perjury on the witness stand in this Court when they said under oath that the Defendant was aware or involved in their drug activity.

Defendant would like to point out to the Court that only the Plaintiff, Patricia Xxxxx and others were arrested and convicted or pled guilty to the charges. Richard Xxxxxs' involvement is unknown but Fabian Xxxxx avoided the arrest somehow and yet he stated on the witness stand that the Defendant was aware of <u>their</u> drug activity. Note, he cleared the Defendant and left him out of involvement by saying that the Defendant "was aware of what <u>we</u> were doing!", therefore admitting his guilt but he has never charged for these crimes, yet.

Plaintiff to this day continues to try to extort the Defendant!

And to this day, after trying to help her over and over get off drugs and clean up her life and giving her a place to stay and eventually divorcing her 15 years ago, she continues to try to extort money from Defendant, usurp his home and extort him into giving her everything he has worked all his life to acquire, his retirement. Defendant is 65 years old. Defendant has recorded threats of extortion from both Tami, Plaintiff, and her brother Calvin wherein they are demanding that he better give her the home and property or they have social security numbers and will make claims to the IRS and other threats, which they left on the

answering machine identifying themselves with the time and date from the phone company, Qwest, on the recording and their phone numbers. Recording available – exhibit Y.

And now Plaintiff has Defendant in court over his house before the same County Attorney who, according to Tami said, "it's a good thing that you took the plea bargain like I did because the County Attorney said he was going to have your ass and prosecute you to the fullest." I swear that is what she said and if I can find the tapes of some of her conversations during 2004 I will give them to the Court! This was when she beat the Defendant with the rake in January 2004 and claimed ownership of the home long before she extorted the Defendant into giving her an Agreement proving she schemed to get the home at least as far back as Jan. 2004, exhibit X.

The following is a brief rundown on what Tami S Keeling and her gang of people, her posse as she calls them, have done since early 2008:

Tami S Xxxxx, Plaintiff, has exhibited that she has no intention of following the law. And, according to the Supreme Court case lookup record also uses: Tammi, Tammy, Tami Xxxxx, Tami Xxxxx, Tami S KXxxxx and just plain Tami KXxxxx without the S, plus Tami Sue KXxxxx.

Tami S Xxxxx, Plaintiff, according to the occupants of the home in the Injunction Against Harassment, J-1102-CV-200802799, threatened them with blowing heads off when she arrived at their home on the 6th of December with several other people for no legal reason whatsoever trying to throw them out of the house which this Injunction was granted with a stern warning to Tami S Xxxxx by His Honor Judge Bain of the Casa Grande Justice Court.

Tami S Xxxxx, Plaintiff, has on numerous occasions attempted to take the law into her own hands by bringing a gang of people with her to forcefully take the home which in doing so not only placed the lives of her gang of people in jeopardy but also placed the lives of innocent people and Sheriff's Officers in jeopardy as the Sheriff's Officers arrived with guns drawn as evidenced by documents filed by Tami S Xxxxx, Plaintiff, with the Court and in Sheriff's Officers reports in which she was complaining about the Sheriff's actions to the Court and by the following police reports:

08002046	**080516134**	**080515073**	**080524130**
080524080	**080514124**	**081019115**	**080929110**
08009706	**081206056 and more, exhibit BB.**		

Order of Protection J-1102-CV-200802203 against Tami S Xxxxx by M Turney and Monica and since this order was issued she has violated it numerous times, exhibit G.

Injunction against Harassment J-1102-CV-200802799 Including threats of great bodily harm where His Honor Judge Bain sternly warned Tami S Xxxxx that he would have her arrested and she would stay in jail for a long, long time, without bond, if he has evidence that she violated the Court Order, exhibit F.

Also as mentioned earlier the Defendant bought at the demand of the Plaintiff a one (1) ton dually truck from L G Xxxxx that was given to the plaintiff, Tami S Xxxxx by the defendant and Monica as additional payment for her extortion which cost $8,500.00 and a situation surrounding that vehicle which was given to Plaintiff at the same time as the $7,000.00 check that plaintiff admitted receiving in Court which stated as a memo "payment in full", truck, exhibit W + Z.

The plaintiff, by filing the matter before the Court, defrauded the defendant for the amount he paid for the truck.

More regarding the truck: Defendant and Monica were called recently by a Sergeant Ellsworth, I believe from the Sheriff's Office, about the truck because our telephone number was somehow on the record as the contact number for Tami S Xxxxx, Plaintiff, and he stated that the one ton dually was impounded towing a trailer which contained a burned out vehicle that had

<u>been used in a HOMICIDE in Phoenix</u> and they were trying to contact Tami S Xxxxx and we informed him that she didn't reside at our home and that this was our phone number.

We might also point out that the 1996 Chevrolet Pickup 3500, one ton dually, with VIN Number 1GC Xxxxx 7845 that Defendant bought from L G Xxxxx is the same vehicle and that Defendant went to the DMV in Casa Grande Arizona on December 15, 2008 in an attempt to get documents showing the transfer of ownership in the truck to Tami S Xxxxx and DMV would not release the information because the owner of record is Tami Xxxxx and to release it is against department policies but I am certain the Court could acquire the documents from the DMV if it so desired.

There was testimony in Judge Olson's court by Tami S Xxxxx, her witnesses Patricia Xxxxx, Richard Xxxxx and Fabian Xxxxx to which they admitted while testifying that they were involved in drug running, money laundering, conspiracy to commit those acts and using the house to run drugs out of which subjected Defendant and Citi Mortgage to seizure from drug enforcement agencies and what with all the criminal activity occurring at the home such as firing Ak47's, pistols and other activities of a violent nature, all of which were subjecting Defendant, Monica, their two children, neighbors and others to harm or death, which are all a proven matter and court record in the Casa Grande Justice Court

during Order of Protection and Injunction Against Harassment trials.

The Defendant asks the Court to consider the following document filed by the Plaintiff in this Court and the evidence submitted along with the testimony of the witnesses for the Plaintiff which prove many false statements and fraud by the plaintiff, exhibit X,:

In the Motion filed by the Plaintiff on CV200801499 date stamped by the Clerk on 08 Aug 11 AM 11:41 the Plaintiff repeatedly lied as proven in the trial held on December 3, 2008 before this Court. In review of this filed document: exhibit X.

The Defendant and the Plaintiff never "had an on going battle over this property for quite sometime" as she stated. Evidence and testimony in the Court proved the Plaintiff never had any claim to the property in January 2004 or during the time that she claims they lived together as husband and wife. The Defendant allowed her to live there in a bedroom proving they did not live as "husband and wife" as she states and that her claim was all in her drug induced imagination and that she, Annette and her two children stayed in "her room". Evidence proves that she claimed the home belonged to her as early as January 2004 and that she Extorted Defendant into an Agreement later in 2004.

She also says "we were trying to leave the home (Annette, her daughter Maria and I)"….. This incident took place during the week and the next day was a school day for Maria and the school bus picked her up very early at the corner of Xxxxx Road and Xxxxx Road. What kind of a parent would be leaving the home at 23:30 hours which is the time stated on the Sheriffs' Report dated 01-11-04, see <u>exhibit N, O and P.</u> And the following paragraphs.

Evidence submitted proves they were drugged up, high on meth, lights on, music playing, talking loud and beating the child and telling her to "go to sleep" behind the dead bolted bedroom door and the Defendant yelled through the door and asked "how can she go to sleep while you are hitting her?" and that if they didn't stop he was going to call Child Protective Services on them and they stormed out telling Defendant that he was going to jail. The filed document proves there was a disagreement on January 11, 2004 and that it was over their abuse of the child.

Annette Xxxxx was a drug abuser and one of her friends at the time was trying to take her kids away from her because of the drug use by Annette. Her sister Rana Xxxxx would not let Annette stay with her because, as she told the defendant at the time, the Sheriff was always stopping her car and searching it because of her involvement with drugs. The Plaintiff moved Annette into the Defendants house without his permission and wouldn't let the Defendant make her move and they dead bolted the bedroom door

so they could do drugs behind his back while the kids were in the room.

Evidence submitted proves she was still lying when she says that she got hurt, the police arrived, and the ambulance arrived and took her to the hospital. Prima Facia evidence proves she hit him with a "stick" as the officer says and she says they were in a "pushing match" and she admitted hitting the Defendant with a "stick". Obviously she lied in the document filed and didn't mention her knocking Defendant out and beat him with a rake and didn't get charged with Assault With A Deadly Weapon, she wasn't born with the rake attached to her body, exhibit N, O + P, and evidence submitted proves she didn't hit him with a little "stick", she beat him with the rake as she admitted she did, exhibit N, O + P.

Exhibit X continued.

The Plaintiff in the document did admit, in the second paragraph of the document, that the County Attorney wanted to prosecute the Defendant confirming that she told the Defendant, "it's a good thing that you took the plea bargain like I did because the County Attorney said he was going to have your ass and prosecute you to the fullest" and at the least, indicated that the County Attorney could have made that statement and that she, the Plaintiff, did in fact tell the Defendant that the conversation

between her and the County Attorney did occur, but who can believe anything the Plaintiff says when evidence proves that so much of it lies.

And, in the same paragraph proved that she claimed she owned the home as early as January 2004, by saying that she got a restraining order against the Defendant which allowed the Plaintiff to take possession of his home, business, files, names, addresses, computers and everything he had and used them to EXTORT the Defendant into the Agreement she say, in the next paragraph, she got on April 24, 2004.

She continues in this filed document to lie by saying that she gave the Defendant 14,000.00 on March 3rd, 2005 and $5,000.00 on March 3rd, 2005 and $760.00 on March 5th, 2005 and $30,000.00 on March 23rd, 2005. There was no evidence to the claimed 14,000.00 whatsoever. And, she testified in Court that the checks she claimed to have given the Defendant that were signed by the deceased Tim Xxxxx years after his death on non-existent checking accounts were never cashed and prudently thinking, why would Defendant take checks signed by a dead person for any type of security? He wouldn't! One of the checks was on her personal non-existent checking account and it was signed by Tim Xxxxx years after his death. The Defendant did not take or hold these checks! And, the filed document claims a $30,000.00 payment which evidence, the receipt, proves was only for $20,000.00.

The Plaintiff, in this filed document included a Certificate of Death showing Tim Xxxxx died on March 23, 2001, confirming that she forged the checks that she claimed to have given to the Defendant including her personal check dated in 2005.

The testimony by the Plaintiff and all of her witnesses, prove that they were involved in drugs, which she admitted in this filed document, X, saying, November 2004, "I was arrested in KY" And, on May 10th, 2005 "I was re arrested for pretrial violation". The re arrest was for failing the prohibition against using drugs! They are drug users as well as drug dealers! Proving that the Defendant just felt sorry for her and tried many times to help her clean herself up and get off of the drugs.

And, in this filed document goes on later to complain about the police showing up and they, the Plaintiff and her posse as she calls them, were "at gun point" proving that she criminally takes the law into her own hands and did not pursue any purported claim in the Courts as the law requires of everyone and in doing so placed the lives of Sheriff Officers and many people in danger.

Then, this filed document shows that she tried to avoid any obligation to the Defendant by filing "July 9th filed chapter 13 bankruptcy" which was later dismissed by the Bankruptcy Court for her failure to file proper documents which proves that she owed

the defendant the money claimed in the bankruptcy papers or else she lied to that court also.

All of the lies in just this one document filed with the Court prove she will lie and if she will lie in one document she will lie in all of the documents and to the Court and in her testimony.

This filed document proves and the testimony on the stand by the Plaintiff and all of her witnesses prove, beyond a doubt that she used the house for unlawful and criminal activity subjecting the Defendant to seizure by the DEA and the Defendant has a right to protect his and Citi Mortgages' interest in the property by evicting admitted unlawful and criminal activity.

This filed document proves that she was in prison, that the Defendant served notice to do repairs and take care of their animals as proven by the dead dog on the chain without food and water and to stop using the property for unlawful purposes on, according to the Plaintiff, "my fiancé", who was Fabian Xxxxx and testimony by her witnesses prove they voluntarily vacated the property instead of doing the repairs. It proves that she gave authority over any claim, rental agreement, or, other claims to her fiancé Fabian Xxxxx and when he vacated the property he did so with her approval and authority to do so as if he were her and acted in her behalf.

The newly discovered evidence and the evidence of fraud and extortion were only ascertained after all due diligence in searching box after box and file after file of stored material that consisted of over 1,200 square feet of items stacked to the ceiling could not have been presented at the trial plus the evidence regarding the truck and the APS bill were only gained after the trial, <u>exhibits A thru BB</u>.

OTHER REASONS JUSTIFYING RELIEF FROM THE OPERATION OF THE VERDICT

THE Xxxxx FAMILY

The defendant feeling certain legally and morally that there was no doubt that he owned the house entered into a sales agreement with the Xxxxx family in March of 2008.

Paul and Suzanne Xxxxx lived in Michigan and wanted a home in Arizona and Suzanne's' sister contacted me and came by to look at the house and took photographs to send to her sister and Paul. After they received the information from Suzanne's' sister they wanted to buy the house and we reached an agreement.

They paid a down payment and were in route from Michigan and Monica and I went on our vacation which was planned for several months.

This was all concluded prior to any claim by the plaintiff that she had an agreement to purchase the home and which as presented in prior grounds above was gained by extortion and fraud and not filed and was violated under numerous terms of the agreement by the plaintiff and terminated by violation and voided by agreement when the plaintiff took the check for $7,000.00 and the One Ton Dually Truck, exhibits W + Z.

They arrived and after conflict with the plaintiff moved into their house.

The Xxxxx family has spent thousands and thousands of dollars making the home into what they want to live in, against the advice of the defendant.

The defendant does not want to see Paul and Suzanne Xxxxx being ordered to vacate the home they call theirs. Paul has been in the hospital numerous times lately and Suzanne is not well either. They have moved from their home in Michigan to this home and would be displaced if ordered to move from the home.

In fact, the defendant offered during the hearing with the Court on February 13, 2009 as His Honor is aware of to settle with the plaintiff for $40,000.00 that Paul and Suzanne Xxxxx have agreed to pay for the equity in the home but the plaintiff refused on record to accept the offer.

Even though the defendant cannot afford to not receive the payments on the $40,000.00 that he offered to the plaintiff during the hearing on February 13, 2009 he feels that the greatest harm would be to Paul and Suzanne Xxxxx emotionally, physically and financially if the Court were to rule in favor of the plaintiff getting possession of the house.

If the Court does not grant a new trial the defendant moves the Court to order a monetary judgment instead of forcing Paul and Suzanne Xxxxx to move from their home which would place an undue hardship on the Xxxxxs'.

OTHER REASONS

In addition, the defendant asks the Court to consider the safety of the defendant in light of the criminal activity by the plaintiff and the threats as proven by Order of Protection and Injunction Against Harassment and the safety of Monica and our two kids and others who may visit or stay with us since the house in this matter is located next door to our home, exhibits F + G.

MONICA, who was brought into this case/matter by threats from the Plaintiff, is very aware of the Failure to protect by those empowered to protect!
See the Order of Protection to protect her from the threats by the Plaintiff, J-1102-CV-200802203 as exhibit attached and see the next paragraphs.

Monica's' Grandfather, who was a Court Constable and retired GM worker and her Grandmother were both MURDERED in their early 60's when the Courts and those in authority FAILED TO PROTECT them after several complaints to those in authority! Monica and her family took the case to the MEDIA, filed a lawsuit against those elected officials and the County/State and won! Their case caused the laws, Nationwide, to change as States recognized they had been empowered and were OBLIGED TO PROTECT INNOCENT PEOPLE! Exhibits not attached for privacy purposes but are available for the Court.

THE PLAINTIFF and her gang are a dangerous and violent group! And, if the Court allows Tami S Xxxxx, the plaintiff, and her gang of people to live right next door to the Defendant, all of us who are trying to stay away from the Plaintiff out of fear, the Court will be subjecting Defendant or other innocent people to being killed by the Plaintiff and her gang of people! Exhibits F + G.

The defendant also asks the Court to consider the fact that the Plaintiff, because of her trying to illegally and forcefully take possession of the house and not using the legal system, has caused the Defendant financial hardship by forcing him to stop his financial endeavors so that he could protect his interest, the interest of Citi Mortgage and the interest of Paul and Suzanne Xxxxx who live in the home and the defendant has paid thousands of dollars in attorney fees and other expenses and is not financially able to pay his bills without the income from the Xxxxxs'.

The defendant asks the Court to consider, if the Court determines that the Plaintiff has a claim to the home, that the determination does not mitigate the crimes and the endangerment of the Sheriff's Officers when they responded "with guns drawn" and other innocent people by the Plaintiff's criminal acts when she took the law into her own hands, several times, by not pursuing this matter in the Court, legally, from the beginning, exhibits F, G + BB.

Instead of legally pursuing the matter the Plaintiff chose, as proven with prima facia evidence – the many police reports – to exhibit a criminal mentality by showing up with a gang of people, using force, threats of great bodily harm, threats of death and more, to forcefully take possession of the home.

The defendant asks the Court to not condone or endorse such criminal actions by allowing the Plaintiff to prevail in the matter before the Court or at the very least to grant a new trial so that a proper, just and legal determination may be made by the Court.

And, why did the Plaintiff wait two years after her release from Federal Prison? It wasn't because the home was occupied as she testified in the Court proceedings on December 3, 2008! A prudent person would realize that she could have started legal proceedings even if the home was occupied! The Defendants' theory, based on his knowledge of how the Plaintiff thinks, is the Plaintiff waited until she was informed by her gang, Richard Xxxxx, Kim Xxxxx and others who live near the Defendant, that the Defendant had left town on a trip. They seized that opportunity to usurp the home, in Defendants' absence, which they thought would be without challenge, not knowing that the Defendant had already sold the home and property. They thought they would all be together again, have a free place to live and do or sell drugs and would force the Defendant to use the legal system to evict them which could take years.

ISSUE: THE
"REAL ESTATE OFFER AND ACCEPTANCE AGREEMENT"
ITSELF, exhibit E.

The plaintiff filed and submitted a document which is the matter before this court, the Real Estate Offer and Acceptance Agreement.

Every civil case that has ever been litigated before any court consisted of an agreement between the parties where one party felt the agreement had been violated. These agreements may have been written, oral or implied agreements. In this matter the agreement as agreed between the parties was a written agreement.

An agreement in all cases has terms and conditions that must be complied with by the parties involved.

We need to break the heading of the agreement down into three parts. The first being the portion of the agreement offered by the plaintiff: the Real Estate Offer and the second part being the action taken by the defendant: the Acceptance and the fact that both parties agreed to all the terms of the agreement we have an Agreement.

In this matter the plaintiff brought to the defendant a Real Estate Offer swearing that she would live by all the terms of her offer and asking the defendant if he would accept the offer provided that she will live by each and every one of the terms of her offer.

On the other hand, the defendant read the offer and agreed that provided the plaintiff will live by each and every term of the agreement (Real Estate Offer) for the life of the agreement that he will accept it (Acceptance) and finally, since the offer by the plaintiff is agreeable with the defendant the contract becomes the (Agreement).

An offer is only an offer and the offer includes every term and condition stated within the offer and it is not an agreement unless it is accepted by the party the offer is presented to.

An acceptance is based on the fact that the offer is acceptable in it's entirety and would not be acceptable if just one (1) of the terms within the offer were to be eliminated or perhaps even if the wording within that term was changed to different wording. If this were to have occurred there would not have been an acceptance at all.

Therefore, for this offer and acceptance to reach its' end goal of being a sale each and every term of the offer must have been complied with by the person making the offer (the plaintiff) and when each and every term has been complied with then and only then is the person agreeable to the offer (the defendant) obligated to comply with his portion of the agreement which would be the sale of and transfer of title to the plaintiff.

The person accepting the offer (the defendant) is not obligated to complete his portion of the agreement when the person making the offer (the plaintiff) violates any of the terms and conditions of the offer that she offered in the first place to solicit or entice or to convince the accepting party (the defendant) into being agreeable and accepting and signing the agreement.

In the matter before the Court the plaintiff violated several of the terms and conditions that she used to solicit or entice or to convince the defendant to be agreeable with her offer which formed the agreement between the parties and once the plaintiff has committed a violation of the offer, an offer that the plaintiff made to the defendant in the first place and agreed to not violate, then the defendant is entitled to terminate the agreement for violations by the plaintiff as per the terms of plaintiffs' offer, exhibits P, Q, R, S, T, U, V + D.

When the plaintiff violated and did not honor her portion of the agreement, it would be safe to say, the defendant is not obligated to honor his portion of the agreement, that being to sell her the house and under the terms of the offer, the offer the plaintiff made to the defendant, the agreement became a rental agreement with a right to evict as per the terms of the offer by the plaintiff and the defendant acted properly when they abandoned the home after being notified to do repairs, clean up the trash and

take care of their animals by serving an eviction notice and in fact that is what transpired in this matter, exhibit E.

In fact, both parties to an agreement must comply with the terms of the agreement. If that were not true then anyone could buy a car and agree to make payments of three hundred dollars a month and then decide to only pay fifty cents a month and the finance company could not repossess the car or they could violate any condition of the agreement and not be subject to repossession. That can't be true and is not the case. They must comply with all terms of the agreement.

The plaintiff violated terms of the agreement as proven by the evidence and plaintiffs' testimony in the trial court that they were using the home for unlawful purposes, admitted drug running and dealing, violating term and condition # 16 of the agreement, exhibit E.

The agreement that the plaintiff felt didn't apply to her is the same offer she made to the defendant and agreed to not violate when she got, by extortion, him to sign the agreement.

And, the plaintiff violated other terms of the agreement such as #8 keep it insured; keep it free of damages; #9 if payment should become more than 30 days late this agreement shall become null and void; buyer may be evicted; and, #16 not store vehicles,

scrap on the land, as the exhibits prove, exhibits D, E + V.

In fact when the notice was served on the plaintiff that they must comply with the agreement and that they are in violation of the terms and conditions of the agreement by having a dead dog on a chain, trashing the yard with old vehicles and scrap, not repairing the roof, windows and broken doors and not insuring the home, they voluntarily chose to move out, abandoning the home, rather than to comply with the agreement. And, by doing so created additional damage by people breaking in and doing damage and leaving drug paraphernalia lying around forcing the defendant to pay the payments to get caretakers to stay in the home who were told to call 911 if those drug addicts show up again.

And that should have ended the matter. The person making the offer in the first place, the plaintiff, violated the very heart of the matter which is the Real Estate Offer, the agreement that she used to solicit or entice or convince the defendant into being willing to sell the house to her at a future date (30 plus or minus years) provided she complied with each and every term and condition of the agreement and of course which she gained by extortion.

After the plaintiff was released from prison she waited almost two years before she decided to usurp the home while defendant was on vacation and the plaintiff recorded the agreement four years after it was initiated and which was violated

by the plaintiff and was terminated when she took the $7,000.00 and the truck, exhibits W + Z. She waited because she knew they had agreed to terminate the matter when she took the truck and $7,000.00.

Once the plaintiff recorded the agreement and filed with the Court the defendant recorded the notice of violation and termination of the agreement,
Exhibit D.

Then the plaintiff decided to forcefully take the house as proven by the numerous police reports listed in this motion.

In addition, the defendant would like to reiterate the fact that the agreement was only consummated because of EXTORTION and FRAUD and that the defendant would never have agreed to the Agreement under normal circumstances and fought against the agreement until it was proven that the plaintiff was destroying his property, files, records, business, computers and was threatening to sue the defendant for claiming to have gotten hurt on his property (the home in this matter) and gained possession of defendants property by lying to Judge Goodman who issued an order preventing the defendant from going on his own property in January 2004, exhibits M, N, O, P, Q, R, S, T, U +V.

And, the plaintiff continues to extort the defendant via telephone calls and with her own testimony in this Court on December 3, 2008 and again on February 13, 2009 during the hearing by threatening the defendant in her statements to the Court that she will initiate further action against the defendant. The statements by the plaintiff are a matter of record on the trial transcripts and stenographers' minutes and recordings if the trial is recorded, exhibit Y.

ERRORS

1. The Court allowed, over the objections of Defendant's Counsel, letters from the Plaintiff that had nothing to do with the case over the continuing objection of the attorney for the defendant which were never substantiated;

2. According to the plaintiff the County Attorney who is at the time Judge Olson, wanted to prosecute the Defendant in a case involving both the Plaintiff and the Defendant where the Plaintiff in this case had beat the Defendant with a rake and officers were called in January 2004 and both were cited for Domestic Disturbance. The Plaintiff stated in the document filed with the Court that the County Attorney, who was Judge Carter Olson, wanted to prosecute the Defendant in this case and the officers statement says that Defendant in this case who was the victim in

the DV case – did not want to prosecute the Plaintiff in this case for beating him with the stick. Defendant knows he can't win with 2 women saying he hit her. Both pled guilty in exchange for a dismissal after domestic violence classes and Defendant in this case participated, whereas the Plaintiff in this case did not and was in violation of court orders for the 2004 case. According to Defendants counsel the Plaintiff was asked if she objected to Judge Olson presiding over this case and the Defendant was never asked if he objected; exhibit X, plaintiff documents.

4. The Court did not properly address that the Plaintiff was paid in full when she signed and cashed the $7,000.00 check which she testified that she did in fact receive and cash and the agreement that she was paid in full for the payments she claims were made by her for the last quarter of 2005 and all payments during 2006 and the Defendant also gave her a one ton dually pickup for any other claimed payments and the Court should apply the $7,000.00 toward the 2005 and 2006 payments thereby negating the ruling that the defendant moved people into the house when there remained prepaid payments, which is in fact, not the case. The Court has not addressed the credit for the $7,000.00; exhibit Z.

5. If the Court were to order the Defendant to sell the home to the Plaintiff the Court would ordering the Defendant to Violate a Contract with City Mortgage which will subject the Defendant to foreclosure, when in fact City Mortgage told the Defendant that the

mortgage must be paid in full unless the purchaser qualified for the full amount of the balance owed on the mortgage with a new loan application which the Plaintiff has proven that she cannot qualify for; exhibits A, B, C + X.

6. The Plaintiff stated in court that she was out of prison for two years and did not take action to claim the house was hers during all that time because she stated that she couldn't take the house because it was occupied. The Plaintiff proved to the court that she is criminally inclined when she tried to forcefully take the house when the Court System was in place for her to file her claims and get a court determination of ownership immediately upon release from prison even though the house was occupied – which she did not attempt to do. In the act of criminally trying to take the house she subjected the officers and everyone else to getting hurt and took the law into her own hands; trial transcripts + exhibit BB.

7. Further to substantiate the criminal intent of the Plaintiff on December 6, 2008 the Plaintiff and several of her friends showed up at the subject house and according to Suzanne Xxxxx threatened her and she initiated a call to the 911 and officers told the Plaintiff to leave and the occupants were told to seek an Order Of Protection against the plaintiff because of the threats and the occupants did ask for and receive an order against harassment against Plaintiff; exhibit F.

8. The Court did not take into consideration that the Plaintiff was using the home for unlawful purposes, drug dealing and money laundering, subjecting the property to seizure by the DEA or other drug enforcement agencies which is a violation of the Agreement and plaintiff and her witnesses admitted under oath; <u>trial transcripts.</u>

9. The Court erred by ruling that the Xxxxx's payments are to be credited to the Plaintiff and in so doing would possibly make the plaintiff liable to the Xxxxx family for the improvements they have made to the house; <u>trial transcripts.</u>

10. The Court did not address the issue of the damages to the home and property after the plaintiff abandoned the property as proven with many photographs filed with the Court. When the defendant assumed his rightful duty to protect the house and property and he spent thousands of dollars doing repairs and cleaning up the property and the plaintiff and her witnesses admitted in court; <u>exhibit T, U + V.</u>

11. Defendant asks the Court whether there are laws that a criminal cannot profit from their criminal activity and the Court would be allowing her to profit from the admitted drug dealing activity which was confirmed on the stand by the Plaintiff, her witness' Richard Xxxxx, Patricia Xxxxx and Fabian Xxxxx; <u>trial transcripts.</u>

12. The Court should consider that the Plaintiff has a million dollar judgment and lien on her by the Federal Court which may subject the home and property to seizure and sale by the Federal Courts;

13. The Court erred in addressing the receipt for $20,000.00. The receipt said "to be decided" because of the delinquency of the Plaintiff the $10,000.00 was credited to past delinquent payments and a few future payments. The receipt is for a total of $20,000.00! In fact, the receipt breaks down into $9,880.00 for 13 payments plus late charges as agreed in #9 of the agreement and there is a notice in the box provided that the defendant is to "see acct" to determine where the money should be applied and any remainder is to future payments; exhibit AA. Defendant would like to ask for an accounting to show how any monetary award would be applied; and

14. Defendants attorney Howard Xxxxx placed a continuing objection to the items the plaintiff presented to the Court and the items were allowed into evidence by the Court, trial transcripts; and

15. The defendant asks the Court to review the transcripts for the trial on December 3, 2008 and in doing so will see that His Honor Judge Olson on more than a few occasions had to wake up the attorney for the defendant by asking him if he was going to object

to an item the plaintiff wanted entered into the record and it was obvious that attorney Xxxxx couldn't hear and the hearing device given to him by the bailiff didn't work and that he was tired and sleeping; <u>trial transcripts.</u>

16. The defendant asks the Court to recognize that according to the plaintiff she received advice and leniency by the Court and that the defendant did not receive any advice or leniency and did not have any representation by anyone as his attorney was ill and inefficient and that the defendant was deprived of a fair trial.

17. The defendant asks the Court to review the hearing on February 13, 2009 wherein the plaintiff again threatened the defendant with threats of taking everything he owned in Court and lied under oath to the Court when she stated that the plaintiff and defendant were together for 18 years. Evidence presented to the Court in this motion and which will be proven with a New Trial show that the defendant divorced the plaintiff in 1994 and she didn't live with the defendant for quite some time and later she was allowed to move into a room when the defendant was trying to help her with her drug problem and the plaintiff didn't live at the defendants home for some time in the late 1990's when the plaintiff moved to Texas and then, once again, he allowed her to move into a room in the late 1990's to help her with her drug problem and that plaintiff beat him with a rake in 2004 when the plaintiff apparently got back involved with drugs as evidenced by her conviction and

time spent in federal prison and the defendant has never allowed plaintiff to occupy any bedroom in any home where he lived since then, hearing transcripts.

18. In the telephonic hearing held on February 13, 2009 at approximately 10:00 AM the defendant explained to the Court that he had newly discovered evidence that was presented in Notice of Superior Claims that he could not have discovered with due diligence prior to the trial.

And, defendant asks the court to reconsider the permissive Counterclaim filed by the defendant on January 26, 2009.

And, the defendant asks the court to reconsider the Motion to Alter Payment Record filed with the Court for newly discovered evidence that could not have been presented at the trial and that while checking the electric use record at APS, they gave him the record from 2004 through 2005 which showed the plaintiff usurped The defendants name and identification and had electric put in defendants name. Evidence submitted as exhibits attached to the Motion to Alter Payment Record.

RELIEF

The Defendant asks the Court in the interest of Justice and to prevent a miscarriage of justice to alter or amend the verdict or to dismiss the above entitle and numbered proceeding with

prejudice or to grant a New Trial.

Dated this ________ day of _________________, 2009.

M. Turney

____

Xxxxx M. Turney, in Pro Per

Xxxxx

Xxxxx

Copies of this Motion for New Trial mailed

This ______ day of ____________2009, to:

Hon. Robert Carter Olson

Judge of the Superior Court

Post Office Box 946

Florence, Arizona 85232-0946

IN THE SUPERIOR COURT OF THE STATE OF ARIZONA

IN AND FOR THE COUNTY OF PINAL

TAMI S. Xxxxx,) **No. CV200801499**
)
Plaintiff,)**Hon. Robert Carter**

v.)**Olson**
)**Division 9**

M. TURNEY,)
Defendant.) **ORDER**
)
______________________________________)

ORDER

Upon the filing and reading of the foregoing Motion for New Trial and it appearing that the said Motion complies with court rules and law, it is hereby

ORDERED, that The Defendant is entitled to____

____________________________________, and

IT IS FURTHER ORDERED, that the above entitle and numbered proceeding is hereby ____, and

IT IS FURTHER ORDERED,

____

____.

DONE IN COURT this _______ day of ____________, 2009.

____

JUDGE OF THE SUPERIOR COURT

Keep in mind; you have to type and file everything, the judge doesn't do anything, including the proposed Court Order for the Judge to sign, apparently, unless they like you or want to do you a favor, or for whatever reason.

I apologize for the repetitiveness but that is the way the system works. I will try not to do that again.

Chapter 23

"In general, the art of government consists of taking as much money as possible from one party of the citizens to give to the other. .... Voltaire (17 64)"

On the same day, February 17, 2009 I filed an application for order of a new trial:

M Turney

In Propria Personna

Xxxxx

Xxxxx

Xxxxx

IN THE SUPERIOR COURT OF THE STATE OF ARIZONA

IN AND FOR THE COUNTY OF PINAL

TAMI S. Xxxxx,	)	**No. CV200801499**
Plaintiff,	)	**Assigned to Hon. Robert Carter Olson Division 9**
v.	)	
M. TURNEY,	)	
Defendant.	)	**APPLICATION FOR ORDER RULE 59(a)4**

Defendant, in pro per, moves the Court for an order GRANTING A NEW TRIAL under rule 59(a)4 based on the grounds defendant properly filed Motion For New Trial and presented sufficient proof of Grounds and Newly Discovered Evidence and that defendant with

proper all due diligence in ascertaining could not have presented the evidence at trial held on December 3, 2008.

This application is based upon the files and proceedings, Legal Review and the Separate Statement of Facts prepared and filed herein.

Dated this _________ day of ________________, 2009.

M. Turney

____

M. Turney, in Pro Per

Xxxxx

Xxxxx

LEGAL REVIEW

This Motion for New Trial is legal prior to entry of judgment. Point of Law: A motion for new trial which must be filed not later than 15 days after entry of judgment may be effectively filed prior to entry of judgment. *Farmers Ins. Co. of Arizona v. Vagnozzi (1982) 132 Ariz. 219, 644 P.2d 1305.* and/or:

A verdict having been reached in this matter as the Court has issued a Notice/Order in favor of the plaintiff. Point of Law: Motion for new trial and to set aside verdict and for judgment notwithstanding verdict was sufficient to extend time for perfecting

appeal, though filed after verdict but prior to judgment. ***Associates Finance Corp. v. Scott (App. 1966) 3 Ariz.App. 1, 411 P.2d 174.*** **and/or: Motion for new trial was properly filed after rendition of verdict but before entry of judgment, and, therefore, there was a proper motion upon which to predicate an appeal.** ***Dunahay v. Struzik (1964) 96 Ariz. 246, 393 P.2d 930.***

This Court has the authority to Order a New Trial. Point of Law: Under the Code 1939 provision authorizing court on its own initiative to order new trial at any time not later than 10 days after entry of judgment, read in connection with provision setting forth the grounds for new trial, a motion for new trial after verdict but before entry of judgment and order granting the new trial were not "premature" since the power to grant new trial may be exercised by the court at any time after verdict, decision or judgment and for 10 days after judgment. ***Sadler v. Arizona Flour Mills Co. (1942) 58 Ariz. 486, 121 P.2d 412.***

STATEMENT OF FACTS

All of the FACTS will just be repeating everything I have said in the prior documents so I will not repeat what has been said before on these pages.

I will skip to the RELIEF sought.

RELIEF

Based on evidence presented in the Motion For New Trial, Legal Review and the Statement of Facts contained in this Application For Order the defendant is entitled to a New Trial and Moves the Court TO GRANT A NEW TRIAL AT THE EARLIEST POSSIBLE DATE CONVENIENT TO THE COURT or in the alternative to dismiss the suit and lis pendens against the defendant with prejudice.

Dated this ________ day of ________________, 2009.

M. Turney

____

M. Turney, in Pro Per

Copies of this Application for Order mailed

This ______ day of ____________2009, to:

Hon. Robert Carter Olson

Judge of the Superior Court

Post Office Box 946, Florence, Arizona 85232-0946

And – of course – I had to type the proposed Court Order for him.

IN THE SUPERIOR COURT OF THE STATE OF ARIZONA

IN AND FOR THE COUNTY OF PINAL

TAMI S. Xxxxx,	)	**No. CV200801499**
	)	
Plaintiff,	)	**Assigned to Hon.**
	)	**Robert Carter**
v.	)	**Olson**
	)	**Division 9**
M. TURNEY,	)	
Defendant.	)	
	)	**ORDER**
	)	

ORDER

Upon the filing and reading of the foregoing Application for Order and it appearing that the said application complies with court rules and law, it is hereby

ORDERED, that The Defendant is entitled under the law to Order granting a New Trial.

IT IS FURTHER ORDERED, that a New Trial will be held on the

_________ Day of __________________, 2009 at _______________ AM in Courtroom _______________________________.

IT IS FURTHER ORDERED, that_____________________

____

_______________.

DONE this ____________ day of February, 2009.

____

JUDGE OF THE SUPERIOR COURT

And at the same time I filed a Motion for a Hearing, just in case that was his decision:

M Turney

In Propria Personna

Xxxxx

Xxxxx

Xxxxx

IN THE SUPERIOR COURT OF THE STATE OF ARIZONA

IN AND FOR THE COUNTY OF PINAL

TAMI S. Xxxxx,	**No. CV200801499**
Plaintiff,	**Assigned to Hon. Robert Carter Olson Division 9**
v.	
M. Xxxxx,	
Defendant.	**REQUEST FOR HEARING**

Defendant, in pro per, moves the Court for a hearing wherein the Court may review the evidence for a proper determination on the Motion for New Trial filed this day.

This application is based upon the files and proceedings and the Motion for New Trial and grounds prepared and properly filed.

Dated this _________ day of ________________, 2009.

M. Turney

____

M. Turney, in Pro Per

Xxxxx

Xxxxx

And I had to type the Order just in case.

IN THE SUPERIOR COURT OF THE STATE OF ARIZONA

IN AND FOR THE COUNTY OF PINAL

TAMI S. Xxxxx,	)	**No. CV200801499**
	)	
Plaintiff,	)	**Hon. Robert**
	)	**Carter**
v.	)	**Olson**
	)	**Division 9**
M. TURNEY,	)	

Defendant.) **ORDER**
)
______________________________________)

ORDER

Upon the filing and reading of the foregoing Motion for New Trial and Application for Hearing and it appearing that the said Motion and Application complies with court rules and law, it is hereby

ORDERED, that Hearing is scheduled on the Court calendar for: ______________________________, 2009 at ____________ AM in Courtroom _________.

ORDERED this __________ day of ________________, 2009.

____

JUDGE OF THE SUPERIOR COURT

I had to get all this in before he made a decision on the 23rd of February as he said he would.

Plus, I had to file the notice of errors that have been entered into the court record which somehow could come back to haunt me later, so I got it done and filed on the 23rd.

Chapter 24

"There is no distinctly native American criminal class...save Congress. .... Mark Twain"

M Turney
In Propria Personna
Xxxxx
Xxxxx
Xxxxx

IN THE SUPERIOR COURT OF THE STATE OF ARIZONA

IN AND FOR THE COUNTY OF PINAL

TAMI S. Xxxxx,	)	**No. CV200801499**
Plaintiff,	)	**Assigned to Hon. Robert Carter Olson Division 9**
v.	)	
M. TURNEY,	)	
Defendant.	)	**NOTICE OF TYPING ERROR IN STATUS REVIEW FILED FEB. 13, 2009**

Defendant, in pro per, would like to point out to the Court an error in the hearing record typed and filed February 13, 2009 at 4:11 PM. Exhibit attached. On page 3 the seventh paragraph down from the top, the <u>defendant did not offer what is typed</u>. Defendant offered to pay the plaintiff $1,000.00 a month for 40 months if the plaintiff would settle the matter. The purpose of this offer was to prevent the undue hardship on the Xxxxx family who live in the home, if forced to move, and, is not admittance of any obligation to plaintiff since plaintiff, by extorted, got the Agreement in the matter in the first place and as filed in Motion for New Trial.

Dated this _________ day of _________________, 2009.

M. Turney

____

M. Turney, in Pro Per

Xxxxx

When I filed this notice of error I checked with the clerk to see if the judge made the ruling yet – it was the 23rd! She said no, he hasn't but I kept calling all day and finally was told that the file stated that the judge was going to pull the file on March 16, 2009 for review. Wow, it worked, at least to some degree. He was going to review it and I have some more time to try to do something else if there was anything else that I could do.

Since I have found out how this judge does things and I realize that he doesn't do what he says so I decided to call his assistant on February 27, 2009 and ask if he has done anything.

It sounded like she might have been being honest with me because she said he is reviewing it now and paused then said well not right now, he's in court, but he has been reviewing the file.

I said that I was told that the file was to be pulled on March 16, 2009 for his review and I asked about that date.

She said, ignore that, he could make a decision sooner or even later than that date.

I ended saying that I guess I better call her almost daily to find out if he has decided to grant a new trial or not and she agreed.

Chapter 25

Criminal minds like poison vines will thrive on prison air,

But all that's good within a man will die while he's in there.

My spirit kept saying, "There's something you missed – look and you will find it!"

So I started looking through documents that the plaintiff filed and then I started reading the documents that I filed then I started reading her documents again. Something caught my attention!

It was exhibit E, the Offer and Agreement! I discussed this exhibit at length in the Motion for New Trial in the Other Reasons section and specifically the argument to the court regarding "The Real Estate Offer and Agreement Itself"!

What caught my attention was Tami, the plaintiff, claimed the document was "Exempt". Note the stamp by the Recorders Office in the area of the upper right side of the page: "Exempt ARS 11-1134 B-10", which was exhibit E.

What is B-10? I asked Monica to remind me to stop by the Recorders Office to get a copy of the list of Exemptions.

In a few days we did and I looked at the list while we were still in the office and I couldn't believe it – she committed fraud when she recorded the document. According to the Exemption form it is a Class 2 Misdemeanor – which was exhibit CC.

I went to work and on March 9, 2009 filed with the court clerk the Application for Order and Notice of Additional Fraud and Criminal Activity by Plaintiff.

However, in my ignorance of the law, I asked the judge for a New Trial, or, to dismiss the suit by the plaintiff and attached two court orders, one for each, giving him a choice.

They were already stamped by the clerk as filed and the clerk said I was giving him too many choices, kind of not to me or to anyone for that matter, but I left because I didn't know if I could trust her.

On the way home I thought about that. She's right! So, I went to work on another Application for Order with only one choice: Dismiss the suit, and filed it on March 10, 2009.

Both documents follow but I will not include repetitive items:

M Turney
In Propria Personna
Xxxxx
Xxxxx
Xxxxx

IN THE SUPERIOR COURT OF THE STATE OF ARIZONA

IN AND FOR THE COUNTY OF PINAL

TAMI S. Xxxxx,) **No. CV200801499**

Plaintiff,	))**Assigned to Hon. Robert**)**Carter Olson**
v.	)**Division 9**)
M. TURNEY,	) **APPLICATION**) **FOR ORDER &**) **NOTICE OF**
Defendant.	) **ADDITIONAL**) **FRAUD &**) **CRIMINAL**) **ACTIVITY BY**) **PLAINTIFF**

THE Defendant, in Pro Per, moves the court to acknowledge and review the following additional newly discovered evidence and proof of fraud and criminal activity, by the plaintiff when the plaintiff intentionally and fraudulently, violated A.R.S. s/s 11-1133 and 11-1137(B) of the statutes.

STATEMENT OF FACTS

The defendant after being extorted by the plaintiff entered into what the defendant considered an agreement wherein if the plaintiff complied with the entire agreement for approximately 30 years then and only then would the defendant sell the house to the plaintiff and at the end of 30 years the defendant would have

signed an Affidavit of Property Value.

The plaintiff after agreeing to terminate the agreement and receipt of $7,000.00 and a one ton truck decided to take the house from the defendant criminally.

The plaintiff filed the four year old agreement with the County Recorders Office which was dated 05-24-2004 on 05-12-2008 as document number 2008-044446, exhibit E and the defendant recorded a Notice of Violation and Eviction # 2008-052071, exhibit D.

Upon visiting the recorders office on March 6, 2009 the defendant ascertained that the plaintiff could not produce an Affidavit of Property Value which is required by statutes to be filed along with the sale of property in Arizona.

The reason the plaintiff didn't have the Affidavit was because it was not a sale and the defendant did not sign an Affidavit of Property Value and in 2004 the plaintiff did not ask the defendant to sign one as the agreement was not a sale until all terms were complied with: 30 years of compliance with all of the terms.

The recorders office, according to the clerk on duty on March 6, 2009 would have asked for an Affidavit of Value and since the plaintiff could not produce one she would have asked if the transfer of the property was exempt by law and showed the plaintiff the list of exemptions.

The plaintiff then claimed the transaction was Exempt per A.R.S. s/s 11-1134 B-10, exhibit E as stamped in the upper right hand corner of the document on Page 1.

B-10 states the reason the plaintiff claims an exemption from the requirement of filing the Affidavit of Property Value, which states:

"A transfer from a husband and wife or one of them to both husband and wife to create an estate in community property with right of survivorship."

The defendant would like to point out to the court that the defendant as proven in documents filed with this court on several occasions, specifically exhibit L, that he divorced the plaintiff in 1994, therefore her statement to the Recorders Office when she entered B-10 on the document stating that the exemption was a transfer from a husband and wife was false.

In doing so the plaintiff violated A.R.S. s/s 11-1133 and 11-1137(B) which require all buyers and sellers of real property or their agents to complete and attest to this Affidavit. Failure to do so constitutes a class 2 misdemeanor and is punishable by law.

Defendant would like to point out to the court that the plaintiff filed the four year old agreement without the consent, approval or knowledge of the defendant as it was during her attempt to usurp the house from the defendant and defendant was on vacation on that date,

Exhibit CC.

RELIEF

For the above reasons the defendant asks the court to Grant a New Trial as previously requested in Motion for New Trial or to dismiss the Lis Pendens, with prejudice.

Dated: This 9th day of March, 2009.

M. Turney

____

M. Turney, in Pro Per
Xxxxx
Xxxxx

Copies of this Notice mailed
this 9th day of March 2009, to:

Hon. Robert Carter Olson
Judge of the Superior Court
Post Office Box 946, Florence, Arizona 85232-0946

Tami S. Xxxxx
Xxxxx

Then I had to type the Order for him to sign which isn't printed here.

Chapter 26

If you are wealthy or well educated, or, if you are a relative or friend of the Judge, you most likely will get Justice.

Since I had some more time I determined that I had better get ready for an appeal and prepare some documents for that so I prepared the Notice of Appeal which, by the court rules has to be filed within a specific time limit. However, by requesting a New Trial I extended that time limit by several days according to the Rules of Court.

I also discovered that I should file a Motion to Alter or Amend the Final Judgment and since I fully expect the judge to go ahead and order me to give her the house I spent a lot of time preparing the motion. However, this has to be filed after he makes a Final Judgment.

This would need to be filed, I believe, under Rule 60(c) 1, 2, 3 and 6. If you recall in the hearing on February 13, 2009 the judge was trying to steer me toward this rule.

Also, in order to keep the number of pages down in this book and because the information I filed in the Motion For New Trial is almost identical, except for the first page, I will not put the entire motion in this book.

M Turney
In Propria Personna
Xxxxx
Xxxxx
Xxxxx

IN THE SUPERIOR COURT OF THE STATE OF ARIZONA

IN AND FOR THE COUNTY OF PINAL

TAMI S. Xxxxx, **Plaintiff,** **v.** **M. TURNEY,** **Defendant.)**	**No. CV200801499** **Assigned to Hon. Robert Carter Olson Division 9** **MOTION TO ALTER OR AMEND JUDGMENT Rule 60(c), 1, 2, 3 & 6**

Defendant, in Pro Per, moves the court under 16 A.R.S. Rules of Civil Procedure, Rule 60(c), 1, 2, 3, & 6 to GRANT RELIEF from the Judgment entered on February 23, 2009 in favor of Plaintiff by dismissing the suit and Lis Pendens with prejudice or by granting a New Trial for the grounds listed below, which consist of mistakes and inadvertence, surprise, excusable neglect and newly discovered evidence which with due diligence could not have been discovered in time for trial as well as fraud and extortion by the plaintiff and other reasons justifying relief from the operation of the verdict and undue hardships on the defendant and the occupants of the home, the xxxxxs', the subject property of this matter and to consider the following grounds in making the ruling for a new trial.

The above is all that I will put in this book because it is almost identical to the Motion for New Trial.

Rule 60(c) 1: mistake, inadvertence, surprise or excusable neglect;

Rule 60(c) 2: newly discovered evidence which by due diligence could not have been discovered in time to move for a new trial under Rule 59(d);

Rule 60(c) 3: fraud (whether heretofore denominated intrinsic or extrinsic), misrepresentation or other misconduct of an adverse party; and

Rule 60(c) 6: any other reason justifying relief from the operation of the judgment.

You could re-read the Motion for New Trial if you feel the need to do that as all of these are included in that motion and the above motion.

If he still rules in her favor and against me I have to file the Notice of Appeal.

Chapter 27

The problem with "unjustice": It doesn't affect "them"!

It only affects you and me, "us"!

M Turney
In Propria Personna
Xxxxx
Xxxxx
Xxxxx

IN THE SUPERIOR COURT OF THE STATE OF ARIZONA
IN AND FOR THE COUNTY OF PINAL

TAMI S. Xxxxx,	)	**No. CV200801499**
	)	
Plaintiff,	)	**Assigned to Hon.**
	)	**Robert Carter**
v.	)	**Olson**
	)	**Division 9**
M. TURNEY,	)	
Defendant.	)	**NOTICE OF**
	)	**APPEAL**
	)	

NOTICE IS GIVEN that Xxxxx M. Turney Defendant appeals to the Court of Appeals, Division Two (2) from the Judgment entered on March 24, 2009 in favor of Tami S. Xxxxx Plaintiff.

Dated: This ____ day of March, 2009.

Xxxxx M. Turney

____

M. Turney, in Pro Per

Xxxxx

Xxxxx

Copies of this Notice of Appeal mailed

This ______ day of ____________200___, to:

Hon. Robert Carter Olson

Judge of the Superior Court

Post Office Box 946, Florence, Arizona 85232-0946

Tami S. Xxxxx

Xxxxx

Xxxxx

Please keep in mind, the motions and/or notices may seem to repeat themselves but because of the type of motion it may include new information or even perhaps exclude information filed with the court in a different motion or notice.

In fact, the way I read the rules, if a motion or notice or whatever is denied then everything you say in it (the document itself) cannot be referenced in a different motion or notice and whenever you file another motion you must put everything in it that you want the court to look at and you cannot refer to the other motion that was denied.

This makes everything very confusing and time consuming to me and it is one of those rules, of several if not many rules, that they have added to insure that you must hire an attorney which gives the judge or court absolute power to determine which party wins.

If the judge still rules in her favor I must do everything over again under different rules and new laws for the Appellate Court.

Chapter 28

"The only difference between a tax man and a taxidermist is that the taxidermist leaves the skin. .... Mark Twain"

I filed a document with the court on Dec. 30, 2008 and additional information along with exhibits (photos, documents, court documents, documents from other people, documents that were written by the plaintiff and more).

The exhibits were all numbered but I will not include them in this book and instead will only describe what they were about.

As I stated before I am the Defendant and she is the Plaintiff.

Description of situation surrounding exhibit P and others:

The officer's statement confirms that the Defendant was the Victim. It confirms that Defendant was beaten with a "stick" according to the Plaintiff, but it confirms that the Defendant was hit with an object that the Plaintiff was not born with. It also says the Defendant was intoxicated.

The Defendant was not intoxicated, he was semi-conscious! If the officer had it would not show more than the level of 2 beers as he had drank 2 beers several hours earlier when he stopped work on the house next door. He was not intoxicated! He had just been knocked out once at the door by the Plaintiff! He was again knocked out and severely beaten with a rake by the Plaintiff. Plaintiff later admitted it was a rake! The Defendant was in shock and a state of semi-consciousness! The Plaintiff tried to beat him to death with the rake and even chased him into the house trying to finish the job. Plaintiff and Annette Nexxxx conspired to do great bodily harm to the Defendant and have him arrested for starting the fight as evidenced by threats in the hall before they went outside and by the phone call to 911 by Annette Newxxx prior to the Plaintiff knocking the Defendant out the first time. Actually the beating by the Plaintiff was Assault with a Deadly Weapon and if it were a man he would have been so charged, photos of Defendant taken a few days later, exhibit P.

This photo “P” is of my left hand. Most of the purple had receded by the time photo was taken. This was the first hit with the rake.

As you read in the Motion for New Trial:

“Annette was saying hurry, I assume to the 911 operator and I looked toward her. I seen movement out of my left eye and instinctively stuck up my left hand. Something hit it HARD and it felt broken. I heard something slam down on the porch…whatever she hit me with had broken. I looked at my left hand and grabbed it with my right hand, it hurt.”

Note: all the photos were not taken for two or three days after the attack with the rake.

The next photo is where the second blow hit me. In the head!

“Then I saw movement toward my head again…but I was too late…everything went black. The next thing I know is I was trying to lock the door from the inside of the house and the Plaintiff was pushing on it trying to get in.

I got it locked and shortly thereafter the police showed up while I was in the bathroom looking at my head, face, hand, arms and legs…they were all cut, bruised and bleeding. She apparently beat me unconscious with something and was trying to kill me.”

The photos below are of my arm and leg.

This arm had apparently been struck by the rake handle after the blow to my head and after everything went black so I wasn't even aware of them until I felt aches and pains and started checking for damage by the attack with the rake.

The top photo is the same arm but higher up near my shoulder. Note the knot where she had continued to beat me with the rake handle.

The bottom photo is cuts, abrasions and bruises on the lower part of my arm.

The following photo is where she stuck me with the rake handle in one of my legs and again this occurred while I was unconscious.
Please note: all of these photographs were taken two or three days after I was released from jail and after I had taken a couple of showers and cleaned up and rested at my friends' home.

I'm the one who went to jail and she was allowed to go to my home and got a restraining order to keep me away from my own home!

Do you believe this is Justice?

Do you believe this could ever happen to you?

Do you know that if you let someone stay at your home for a few days they have the same rights to the house as you do and you cannot make them leave if they refuse to go?

You must legally take them to court and evict them and if they fight the eviction it can take months.

And, did you know that if they say you hit them you could get told to stay off your own property by a judge?

Do you know that they have the right while living in your home to invite anyone they want to visit – even if it is someone you can't stand or a drug addict?

Do you know that they all have a right to use the entire home?

Do you know that they can get a restraining order against you and that you can't even go back to your own home until – someday – you win in court? If you win!

It's a fact and if you don't believe me, read my case again.

There seems to be a simple answer to correct the way they do this, at least to me!

Since the enforcement officer at the scene has the authority to make a decision then wouldn't it seem logical that he should make a decision based on some kind of proof or evidence when it's available?

If the officer had asked for proof of ownership, while he was at the scene, the entire issue of the restraining order against me, the owner, would have been avoided and the restraining order would have been against her, not me!

If he would have asked that question I could have showed him my deed and she could not have shown him anything!

This entire case could have been avoided with that simple

question and the deed!

The problem is “unjustice”.

It creates a lot of work and good money for cops, lawyers and judges. And, the courts can keep asking and getting more money to handle their huge case load and more money to hire new judges and more money to build big new elaborate court buildings. Money gives them Power!

The main reason for all of the “UNJUSTICE” in this country is: it establishes a criminal record for about 90% of the population and takes away their right to own a weapon for self-defense.

Chapter 29

“What this country needs are more unemployed politicians. .... Edward Langley, Artist (1928-1995)”

After all this time, fighting the plaintiff and the “unjustice”, the family that I really have an agreement with for the home have become concerned that they may have to move suddenly because of possibly being evicted by the judge so they started looking for another home in the area and they told me that they were just going to move if they can find another home.

When we first met I had mentioned to them that I had an empty lot and they looked at it and really liked it and they had already looked at a manufactured home and really liked it also.

I agreed to give all of their money off of the price of the lot if they wanted to move there with the manufactured home and because of the stress from the plaintiff and the court system and process so we reached an agreement for them to give up the home and move to the lot.

We talked to the attorney that I had fired, just to see what his opinion was on how to handle this and he said you sold it to them with the Rent to Own agreement and you have to foreclose on them to cancel the agreement! What? I asked. We have agreed to terminate the Rent to Own agreement and they are going to take a lot to move a home on and live there.

He said that he would never represent something like this, even though it is mutually agreeable and he said perhaps I need to record the papers for the termination and the new lot agreement myself.

What does this prove? It proves that because of unjustice we cannot make an agreement with someone! We are forced to hire an attorney for everything we do! And, if an attorney didn't write the agreement in the first place, the judge in some court will rule against us and we lose.

They have really got it all messed up and they have gained power and control over every agreement you might make with anyone for any purpose.

And he said that we needed to type up and file an Election to Forfeit and an Affidavit of Completion of Forfeiture just to protect myself against any judge in any court as if they had violated the R T O agreement and I had foreclosed on them.

In fact they had never violated the agreement and we have mutually agreed to terminate the R T O and I agreed to give them money off the lot but, according to the lawyer, if they ever wanted to come back and say they owned the home I would have a problem! Problem, "unjustice"!

The attorney that I fired, Howard, is a good guy and really seems to be a nice person. I have paid him around $9,000.00 for his services which, as you have seen by my firing him after the trial, offered very inefficient representation, he's 82 years old.

I was told by another attorney that I could sue him for malpractice but I haven't decided to do that.

I stopped in his office to discuss the case regarding the Rent to Own agreement above, just to get an opinion, not to retain him.

We were discussing the notices, motions and papers I have prepared and the hours required to type, research, locate evidence and more and I mentioned the one three day weekend where I had put in over 40 hours in those three days.

I said, off the top of my head, "I couldn't ever have been able to afford to use you for all of this! I'll bet it would have cost me $100,000.00 for your service, to do what I have done." He absolutely agreed and he said maybe more by the time you're done.

I was telling him about filing a Motion for New Trial just recently.

He asked if I had put in the motion that the judge was biased or prejudiced against me and I replied that I had and that I said the same thing in one of the other motions but the judge had denied the motion.

He, said "you need to remind him that at the hearing he said he should step down and not preside over this matter because of his personal relationship with the plaintiff and then he (the judge) turned to the plaintiff and asked her if she objected to his presiding over the matter" (case) and she replied that she did not object but he didn't ask the attorney if I objected. Wow! He has a personal relationship with her!

In addition the attorney said that he was at the court talking to someone and the judge said "is that Howard xxxxx?" and came out to talk to Howard. Howard said to the judge "thank you for letting me withdraw from this case" and the judge said that he wished he could find a way out of it! Wow! Prejudice and bias and justice denied!

Tami probably had someone to hold over the judge, and was.

The problem is "unjustice"!

It is now early March 2009 and I decided that I might need some of the documents in the file with the attorney so I called him and asked if I could pick up the file at his office and he said certainly.

We went by his office and he handed the file to me but I took a moment to ask him if he remembered the date of the hearing when the judge said something about his personal relationship with the plaintiff.

He said it would be in the file that he just gave me so I looked through it and found a reference to the “discussion” about the judge and criminal charges in 2004 but there wasn’t any detail about the conversation.

I then asked if he would give me a statement about the discussion and what was said. He thought for a moment and then said that I would have to let him think about that.

He’s never going to do it and the reason is: he’s afraid to make a statement about the judge because he might have to go in front of him at some future date.

Another reason is because if he makes statements in writing I could possibly sue him for malpractice.

So I guess I’m on my own and won’t get any help from him.

I discovered in the Minute Entry, Status Review exhibited earlier in this book and dated 02/13/2009 on page 3 it discusses a hearing on September 8, 2008.

That is the hearing the attorney said the judge made the statement about his “personal relationship with the plaintiff”.

As you will see in the next chapter I have to get trial transcripts for the Court of Appeals and I specifically asked for the transcripts for that hearing. Guess what?

The court clerk said they didn’t have a court reporter at that hearing so there would not be any transcripts!

That’s convenient! – That’s UNJUSTICE in motion.

Chapter 30

"Government's view of the economy could be summed up in a few short phrases: If it moves, tax it. If it keeps moving, regulate it. And if it stops moving, subsidize it. .... Ronald Reagan (1986)"

I have consistently either called the clerk of the court, called the court assistant or went by the clerk counter at the court and asked them to see if the judge has made any decisions regarding the request for a new trial and I keep getting told that he hasn't made any decisions yet.

Since the judge still hasn't made a decision regarding the motion for a new trial I am forced to continue with research and preparation for an appeal.

One of the things needed for an appeal is the trial and hearing transcripts which are the typed record of the proceeding which must be done by the court reporter. The court reporter is the person that sits in front and keeps a record of everything that is said.

I started over a month ago trying to make contact with the court reporter for each hearing and for the trial.

The problem with trying to contact the reporter is that there may be a different court reporter for each and every hearing and/or trial.

I have been given phone numbers by the clerk of the court to contact them and I have called and left messages but I never get a return phone call.

Then I called the phone number again and get someone who says that that particular reported isn't there any longer!

Apparently they take the record with them! What happens if it's lost or they die or move to China? This is crazy!

Finally I got a phone number from someone so I called it. Apparently it is their home so I leave a message. I call again the next day and a lady answers "hello" and I explain to her that I need a transcript and she says he, I assume her husband, will call me back.

He did and said he will get back with me on the cost to prepare the transcript which he did for the two hearings he was involved in.

Another court reporter I had left messages for finally called back also and said she will call back with a price.

She did and wants in the vicinity of $1,000.00 to prepare the transcripts for only one of the hearings and the trial.

I called the clerk and explained that since the typed minutes of the hearing on February 13, 2009 are incorrect and that I filed a notice telling the court that the statements made by the court reporter are incorrect and that I want a copy of the actual courtroom audio tapes and perhaps the video tapes as well!

The clerk said that he will have to get back with me on that request since he has never had that question presented to him before.

He did call me back and said that they cannot give me copies of the video or the audio tapes. They are court property and since not every courtroom has that system, as their court does, it isn't a requirement to furnish them to anyone.

That is interesting! The things they type that goes into the record for the case is wrong! And, you can't get the tapes so that you can make certain that the record is correct!

Plus they don't have transcripts for the hearing on September 8, 2008! Humm!

In late March 2009 I paid for and received the transcripts from one of the court reporters which I will need for the appeal process.

In addition, I have finally made contact with another court reporter and have made arrangements to pay for the two transcripts that she was involved with. Again, I must have all transcripts for the Court of Appeals.

Chapter 31

If the Government wants a population that is content with the Government, then the Government must fix The Unjustice System!

I have a horse in my pasture that is smarter than most of the people in power in this country. And, I don't say that lightly!

If I stretch an electric shocker wire around the pasture the horse will sniff it to see what it is and when she touches it with her nose, zap, she gets an electric shock and jumps back. She doesn't like it!

She is smart enough to know not to touch it again.

On the other hand most of the people in power will never learn from their mistakes and they don't learn anything from history either.

They will keep touching the electric fence over and over again!

Now, I'm not saying this about all of them. Hopefully some of them are intelligent enough to learn from history and learn from their mistakes.

If we, the people, put out some effort to make a change maybe we will start getting people in power with a little more horse sense!

This is my plea to the leaders and to the President, not for myself alone, for the all of the people of this great nation:

Feel free to copy the next pages, put your name at the bottom under mine and mail it to the President, to the Congress, to the Senate, to the Governor or retype it and send it – just send it to all of them!

Dear Mr. President,

Sir,

Please do something about unjustice.

Throughout history governments have never been willing to change the way they abused their power until there was a major problem. Well we have a problem now! Please don't wait for it to become a major one. It's big enough already!

Every country and peoples around the world have a history of prejudice against specific groups of people and so does this country.

Well, I'm black and let me ask you a question. What would you have done in my shoes?

I'm a Jew, what would you have done in my shoes?

I'm a Christian, what would you do in my shoes?

I'm gay, what would you do in my shoes?

I'm heterosexual, are we going to be next on the hate list?

I'm white and this problem is not pointed specifically toward any race, religion or gender! It persecutes 98% of us, me too!

It is rampant and it depends on the race, religion or gender of the person in power, the one who commits the unjustice, because he or she directs their prejudice toward anyone they don't like.

I am in prison and I'm innocent, what would you do in my shoes?

I want a job and can't get one because of my 20 year old prison record, what would you do in my shoes?

There are a lot of innocent people in prison!

A copy of my book "Unjustice" is attached.

We've only touched on a few in this book. Look at the case of Hurricane, the young man in Washington State and the father who was charged with incest. There are millions more in this country alone.

If we can't fix the unjustice system from the bottom up then we need to fix it from the top down but you, the leaders at the top, need to start at the bottom because that is where the 98% of us that are affected the most receive the unjustice and punishment, or, death sentences.

So how do we determine who, out of the millions that have been found guilty and served a sentence in the past or is currently serving a sentence, are guilty?

If there is any doubts of guilt, if they've been fighting their case for years, if after years they are still proclaiming their innocence, if their sentence has already been served and they have not committed any crime after 10, or 20 or 25 years since being released then we need to give them the benefit of the doubt and reverse their convictions.

They were most likely convicted because of prejudice, bias, hate, well, because of unjustice!

And, the problem is not just criminal. If you will just read this book you will see that it is civil as well and I don't have a suggestion as to how to reverse those judgments.

But, I do have a suggestion regarding how to eliminate the wrongful judgments and convictions in the future and that is change the unjustice system, change the rules of court, and go back to the constitution.

You could start today and I am asking you to do that.

I would like to point out something that you may not even be aware of.

With your position and with such great responsibility placed on your shoulders, you count on those in authority that you have appointed or that are elected, to do their jobs correctly.

As you are probably aware, there is an old saying, which is, "the buck stops at the top". You get the blame for everything that goes wrong.

Well, there are a lot of wrongs being done from the lowest level to the highest level.

And as with the master servant law, the master is responsible for the servant in any damage litigation. You're the master, sir.

You are the only one with the power to initiate a change in the Rules of Court, United States Supreme Court, Federal Courts, State Supreme Courts and all lower courts and the law enforcement officers.

You are the only one with the power to take the word "unjustice" out of The Unjustice System and make it a Justice System.

I am asking you to appoint a commission of everyday people to study and work out a better system of justice. Not lawyers, they just confuse the system for money and job security.

I am asking you Mr. President to start the process and to finish it in your time left in office because the next president could be Hitler!

I'm asking you to fix unjustice!

Your Humble Servant,

Mac Turney

Chapter 32

The Constitution was written to protect the people from the power of the Government.

If you don't believe me ask the people who wrote it – the Government back then was the British.

The problem with "unjustice":

It doesn't affect "them"! It only affects you and I, "us"!

You and I consist of roughly 98% of the world population.

The other 2% of the world population are the affluent and well educated that pretty much run the world.

The 2% generally get justice because they have influence and enough money to hire the best attorney. They're well educated and they're able to write and say their cases in a way that the courts accept as well as understanding and complying with the Rules of Court. While gaining their education they probably attended some classes on law as well as classes to get a degree in their chosen profession.

The 98% (us) are not wealthy or influential and are not well educated. We can't afford an attorney, let alone the best attorney.

Due to lack of higher education we are unable to write or say things as the courts want it and we may not even be able to understand what they are trying to say in the Rules of Court.

I'm not saying this to be rude, it's a fact. 90% of the people in prison are uneducated with a low IQ and broke and they are White, Asian, Black, Indian, and Mexican, straight, gay, Methodist, Catholic, and Baptist, Jewish, Islamic and well, you get the point, and 95% of them are men.

The court system, prosecutors and law enforcement tend to use the woman as a witness against the man and they make a deal with her, where she does very little time, or, no time, in comparison to the male even if the crime was her idea and she was the leader of the gang.

This scenario is exactly what happened to the woman, the plaintiff in the case we are discussing in this book.

Two women and several men were arrested for many felony charges revolving around drugs and money laundering. One of those women was the plaintiff. The two women got three years in federal prison for testifying against the men and the men got thirty-five to life.

Then the two women start a new crime spree after they spend a short time in prison, form a gang of people around them, try to steal my house and other crimes and continue with their criminal occupation.

This book is not just dedicated to the scenario above, this case. It is dedicated to "unjustice" which affects the entire 98% of "us" and it doesn't discriminate between male and female. I'm certain there are a lot of innocent females in jail or prison, too!

And, it's all because of "unjustice"!

Chapter 33

I don't care how much you have, where you've been or what you've done. I want to know who you are today and what you will sacrifice for yourself, the people, for justice and for peace

In any case, I thank God I was born in America where I can at least write this book without being imprisoned just for writing it and I can publish this book.

Now I'm not saying that I will not get persecuted or harassed or sent to prison, because I very well might be, perhaps even for something I didn't do, because of this book.

Let's face it, I have stepped on some toes and all it takes is one of those affected by this book to do something and I could be in big trouble.

So why am I doing it? Well, as I said in the beginning, I believe in God and I personally love this country. I was in the military and was willing to die for this country and I still am.

The problem is not the country or the people of the country. Perhaps it isn't even the government. The problem is "UNJUSTICE"! And we, the people, can fix it if we try.

What can we do about it? We can write to congress, write to the President, form groups to gather signatures to mail to politicians demanding a congressional hearing and demand the laws and rules of court get changed so that we have a chance to win when we didn't do anything wrong. ALSO, if you are a juror, demand that the system works the way you know it should by voicing the wrongs done by your verdict. We can also, peacefully, protest.

When you write, tell them we need to go by the Constitution that was written so that all of us can count on justice and equal rights and tell them they all need to honor their pledge to defend the Constitution and recognize they work for us, the people.

One thing that I will add as I am nearing the end this book is the chain of events that guided me through this ordeal could not have been anything other than spiritual.

Even the title, “unjustice” was given to me at 4:11 AM one morning when I woke up saying “unjustice”!

And, the content and words to write this book was started and given to me and just flowed as I typed!

Sometimes we have to go through unpleasant things but if we are walking our life as morally correct as we can and open our hearts, eyes and ears we just might understand what we should do.

The chain of events that occurred to make things fit together was not just coincidences. My wife and I were in the right place at the right time for things to happen that must have been necessary for this case to become a book.

I believe it is meant for you to read, for some reason unknown right now and I believe what you have read will be a blessing to you at some time in your life or the blessing might not be for you at all.

It might be for someone else who would have been wronged because of unjustice and by your efforts to re-establish justice they will be blessed and your personal blessing could be the in knowing that you helped many people.

What you do right now and for some time to come, until we get the court system changed so that there truly is Justice in the justice system, could affect the lives of many people in the future.

Your blessing might be a blessing that you will receive while you are putting forth effort to restore justice or when you realize that your efforts have helped prevent a great wrong that may have been done to someone else that truly doesn’t deserve it.

Maybe your efforts will even save countless innocent lives that would have been spent behind bars; countless innocent lives that would have been spent in poverty because someone cheated them out of all that they worked hard to acquire; lives that could have been lost because of "U N J U S T I C E!"

Chapter 34

Ode to the Innocent Ones:

I don't know how it happened, to me;
But when I look around I find,
The same four walls I'm locked behind;
Many have a criminal mind, I see;
And criminal minds like poison vines,
Will thrive on prison air;

But all that's good within a man,

Will die, while he's in there;

I pray, someday, there's more than this for me

What can we do?

The word "unjustice" is missing from the dictionary and perhaps it needs to remain missing. But now that it actually is a word it may belong there. But, it could be eliminated from our lives if we are willing to put out some effort.

Write your congressman or congresswoman and demand a Congressional Hearing on The Unjustice System;

Write to the President and demand that the Unconstitutional Laws passed by past Presidents be eradicated;

Demand your rights under the Constitution of the United States of America;

If you are on a jury and someone was denied their Constitutional Rights vote them innocent;

You don't have to do what the Judge or Prosecutor says in their instructions to the jury;

Insist that they have proof before you find someone guilty; circumstantial evidence is not proof; the opinions of the prosecutor and many of his witnesses are not proof;

The people who immigrated to America after 1492 did so to escape unjust taxes and illegal persecution and prosecution and they wrote the Constitution to protect themselves (us) from the government that was taxing and persecuting them.

They put in it, the rights to bare arms for protection against their own government, the British!

That right has been taken away from us! And, the next government may be Hitler!

We need to demand that right be restored and demand that we will always have that right.

The British would have lost WWII if private guns from the American Citizens, consisting of hundreds of thousands of guns, were not sent to them.

Your rights to privacy are disappearing;

The right to protection from unreasonable searches and seizures;

The right to a fair trial;

The right to equal justice under the law;

The right to vote is being delegated to the ones they choose to be allowed to vote;

They have been eliminated because of UNJUSTICE;

Your right to protect yourself and your family from harm is being eliminated;

Your right to protect your property is gone;

The right to run your own household in an orderly and morally correct manner is gone;

The right to teach your children work ethics is gone;

The right to teach your children about God is going rapidly;

In fact the right to believe in God is rapidly becoming a criminal act;

And more, and more, and more of our rights are disappearing rapidly.

We need to stop drugs and I'm certain you agree, but we need to end the Declared War on Drugs by, I believe, Reagan.

That Declared War actually puts us under a Declared Martial Law! It needs to end!

We need to insist, demand, that our Constitution be the Law of the Land.

We have a new President every four years and I sincerely believe he will listen when we talk to him or her about unjustice, injustice, injustices, bias, prejudices, and anything along those lines. Most Presidents will listen but will they try to do something about the problem? We have to try, don't we!

Write him! Call him! Email him! Text him! Send him a telegram! Contact him in any way possible and let him know how you feel about unjustice!

And use the web to let the world know how you feel and to keep up with news on unjustice.

We will be trying to keep our website updated on a regular basis so check back often. And, any new information on the case discussed in this book and other cases that users post on the site will be updated as new events occur.

We will also try to maintain links where you may find Laws and Rules of Court.

Also links to Attorneys that appear to sincerely put forth effort on their clients' behalf.

We will also try to maintain a list of services, offered at a discount, to those who can't afford the best attorneys but want the best representation.

If possible, in the near future, we would like to offer a contributors area for contributions to visit with visitors who need legal representation but cannot afford an attorney.

I've always had a saying that I feel is appropriate given the way the country is going and that is: "Bureaucracy, Inefficiency and Drugs will be the downfall of this Country!" And, I have made this statement to many people over the years with the disclaimer, "but, not necessarily in that order".

But, I would like to change that saying now that I am more aware of "unjustice".

My new saying is this: "Unjustice, Bureaucracy, Inefficiency and Drugs are the downfall of this country. But not necessarily in that order"!

Feel free to use this saying anytime you want. It's the truth!

Chapter 35

If you don't believe I am telling you the truth ask any lawyer, judge or politician and they will tell you that I am lying – then you'll know that I am telling the truth.

Please let me say this before I write the ending to the case that we have been discussing:

Whether I win or lose I have to keep trying, legally, to get this loco person away for us and Unjustice fixed in America.

And what matters is that it took this case for this book to be written!

If this had never happened to me it might have taken years for someone else to be inspired to write this book and we would have had many, many more innocent victims of "UNJUSTICE"!

I thank God that it happened to me and that supernatural events during the process caused me to realize that this book needs to be written.

And, I thank God for the words to write this book. I only went to the 8th grade in school. At 12 years old I started working for a living, building homes with my brother who was a contractor and I was a foreman by the age of 15 years old.

Well it is now March 26, 2009 and I received through the mail another Notice/Order from the court. The judge is obviously denying all of my Motions and Applications and is going to rule in her favor but note it is not signed so it is not a final order, not a final judgment.

He is however, setting a hearing to evict the family who are now residing in the house.

Yes, I fully expect him to give her my house with a final order soon!

IN THE SUPERIOR COURT

PINAL COUNTY, STATE OF ARIZONA

Filed In Court Record
Date Filed: 03/24/2009
Time Filed: 02:36 PM

DATE: 03/24/2009

THE HON ROBERT CARTER OLSON
Division: 9

By, Kimerlee Judicial Assistant

TAMI S K , **Plaintiff(s),** vs. **M TURNEY,** **Defendant(s).**	**CV200801499** **NOTICE/ORDER**

The Court **FINDS** no legal basis for granting a new trial. The Court specifically rejects the assertion that Defendant's counsel was ineffective or impaired; the Court expressly disclosed the potential conflict for the Court, both in writing and on the record, and neither party objected or requested a change of judge; and while the Court respects the Defendant's right to disagree with the Court's judgment, the Defendant has not identified a legal basis for a new trial, and the Court's judgment was largely predicated upon admissions made directly by the Defendant.

IT IS HEREBY ORDERED denying the *Motion for a New Trial*, filed February 17, 2009; *Application for Order Rule 59(a)4*, filed February 17, 2009; *Application for Order & Notice of Additional Fraud & Criminal Activity by Plaintiff*, filed March 9, 2009; *Application for Order*, filed March 10, 2009;

Upon a further review of the file, the Court **FINDS** that a Forcible Entry and Detainer was Ordered filed in this Cause by the Maricopa/Stanfield Justice Court, since the ownership of the subject property is in dispute. However, this Forcible Entry and Detainer may not be consolidated with this action, but must be filed in a separate civil case.

IT IS FURTHER ORDERED that the Maricopa/Stanfield Justice Court Forcible Entry and Detainer is not consolidated with this cause.

IT IS FURTHER ORDERED that the Clerk of the Court shall open a new Civil file, without additional charge, and file a copy of the December 31, 2008, filing from the Maricopa/Stanfield Justice Court, and that matter shall be set for Initial hearing on Tuesday, March 31, 2009, at 3:00 p.m., before the Honorable Robert Carter Olson, Division 9. The distribution list for the

5001 CV200801499 Page 1 of 2

new file shall include Tami Ke and Suzanne & Paul , at the addresses shown in the papers submitted by the Maricopa/Stanfield Justice Court.

IS FURTHER ORDERED directing a copy of this Minute Entry be placed in the new Civil File showing the Initial Hearing date of March 31, 2009.

Mailed/distributed copy: 03/25/2009

cc:
TAMI S KE
PO BOX
CASA GRANDE AZ

M TURNEY
PO BOX
AZ

PAUL AND SUZANNE
51759
AZ

CV200801499 Page 2 of 2

And, now it is the next day, March 27, 2009 and I received the following document from the court.

Note that it is signed so it is a Final Judgment.

IN THE SUPERIOR COURT

PINAL COUNTY, STATE OF ARIZONA

Filed in Court Record
Date Filed
Time Filed:

DATE: March 24, 2009

THE HON ROBERT CARTER OLSON
Division: 9

By, Kimerlee Johnson Judicial Assistant

TAMI S K **Plaintiff(s),** **vs.** **M TURNEY** **Defendant(s).**	**CV200801499**

The Court **FINDS** that a valid contract for deed was executed by the parties during May 2004, obligating the Plaintiff to pay a certain amount of consideration, and obligating Defendant to immediately transfer possession of the subject property, commonly known as 51759 , and later to convey good title when the full amount is paid.

The Court **FINDS** that the monthly payments of $760.00 were applied, under the terms of the contract, against principal, interest (7.375% per annum) and impounds; thus, each payment was not applied exclusively against principal, as Plaintiff unsuccessfully argued.

Although the evidence was conflicting concerning the prior payment history and past transactions between the parties, the Court **FINDS** that, on March 23, 2005, Defendant executed a written receipt, which he admits is authentic (Exhibit 24), evidencing a payment of $20,000.00, proof that all future payment obligations were satisfied until June 20, 2006 AND proof of another credit to Plaintiff of $10,000.00, which might later be applied against principal or future payments.

The Court **FINDS** that Defendant took possession of the property on or about December 22, 2005, without consent of Plaintiff or any lawful authority, and converted the property to personal use, by allowing the family of his girlfriend/spouse to reside in the residence for more than two years, followed by another tenancy that continues to this date.

5003 OFFLINE

Page 1 of 3

The Court **FINDS** that Defendant's possession and use of the subject property constituted a breach of the contract, and Plaintiff is entitled to credit for payments in-kind for this period of use. The Court sets the value of that use of the property at the contract rate of $760 per month (or the amount of the gross mortgage payment, whichever is higher), as if the Plaintiff had made a monthly payment in that amount to Defendant each and every month since late December 2005.

The Court **FINDS** that the *Notice of Election to Forfeit* was legally deficient and wholly ineffective, because no amount was unpaid and past due; and at all relevant times, the Defendant was in breach of contract, not the Plaintiff.

The Court **FINDS** that the current loan balance of $78,887.44, payable to CitiMortgage as of November 3, 2008, Account #077 10-3, reflects the current and correct loan balance due after all offsets, except Plaintiff remains entitled to credit for the amount ($10,000.00) that would later be applied against principal or future payments, as well as credit for six months pre-paid rent, for the period between December 22, 2005 and June 20, 2006, when Plaintiff was denied use of the property, although rent was prepaid;

IT IS HEREBY ORDERED that (1) Plaintiff is granted immediate possession of the subject property from Defendant, *subject to any superior claim by any third party*; (2) Plaintiff is awarded from Defendant $14,560.00, plus interest at 7.375 per annum from March 23, 2005, until paid or applied to future payments; and (3) Plaintiff remains obligated to pay consideration, under the terms of the original contract, for the amount that remains due under the existing CitiMortgage loan.

IT IS FURTHER ORDERED that the Defendant shall keep the mortgage current and continue making all payments on the mortgage, as payments in-kind on behalf of Plaintiff, until possession is returned to Plaintiff, such that no payment shall remain unpaid with a due-date of less than thirty days at the time possession is returned.

IT IS FURTHER ORDERED that this is a final judgment, pursuant to Rule 54(b), Ariz.R.Civ.P., and the time for appeal shall begin to run from this date; however, this Court shall retain jurisdiction to grant further relief, if the property is not returned in good condition, or if possession cannot be returned by Defendant to Plaintiff, such as if a third-party has a superior right to the property.

IT IS FURTHER ORDERED vacating all future calendar dates and closing this file.

HONORABLE ROBERT CARTER OLSON

5003 OFFLINE

Page 2 of 3

She won! I am really upset. She is a dangerous person!

Her and her gang can do anything and get away with anything.

She is going to be living right next door to me as soon as they can evict the family from the house! There is a real threat that she may kill me or plant something to frame me or anything. I am concerned!

We need to all do our best to work together and fix the UNJUSTICE system.

Now I have to start the appeal process and there are a whole new set of rules and new laws to look up but I have to do it. This is a dangerous situation.

During all of this I stopped and asked myself a question: “What is the Law?” and, after careful consideration, the best answer I can give is, “the Constitution and the Law are mans’ feeble attempt to do what is right”.

I suppose, once upon a time in the past, the Law was prone to “do what is right” more often than not, except when prejudice or bias entered the courtroom. They’ve always been able to convict anyone because of prejudice or bias!

At one time it took real evidence to convict someone but it doesn’t today. All it takes is circumstantial evidence and professional opinions.

When we add in the problem of “unjustice” we have a much bigger problem because now power comes into play. With Power, Prejudice and Bias the Law can convict anyone, anytime, for no reason and you can lose both criminal and civil cases as well.

Rules of Court and corruption by lawyers to gain power and control deny the average citizen equal access to the courts. Unjustice has destroyed our faith and trust in the system and the government!

Let's hope that someone will listen to our voices and fix The Unjustice System.

Chapter 36

Every civilized country has some sort of written system in place that they use to promote as their system of justice!

This written law or constitution to regulate the justice system is used for propaganda purposes: to make the population - and in fact the world - aware of the fact that there is fairness in the trials and in the punishment of their population.

That may be all that it is: propaganda! And A Lie.

I filed the case in the Appellate Court and while awaiting their decision, which takes months, HER JUDGE evicted the people from the house and let her move back into it.

We don't trust the situation so we stay in another house in town most of the time but check on our house which was 13 miles from where we stay every day and we put in a surveillance system with 6 months of recorded storage for each of the cameras.

After about a year Tami didn't make and payments as the Judge had ordered and we didn't make any payments either. Needless to say Citi Mortgage foreclosed on her and evicted her and sold the house at auction messing up my credit – but I don't care – SHE'S GONE.

This case continued through the Appellate Courts and I continued to lose every step. She Won! But it doesn't end there:

To Be Continued Until UNJUSTICE Is Fixed!

SOME FINAL THOUGHTS:

Every civilized country has some sort of written system in place that they use to promote as their system of justice!

This written law or constitution to regulate the justice system is used for propaganda purposes: to make the population - and in fact the world - aware of the fact that there is fairness in the trials and in the punishment of their population.

That may be all that it is: propaganda!

If the country doesn't have this written system in place it is called a third world country and the rulers are called dictators.

When the country does have a written system in place it is called a civilized country.

If you will notice on the front cover of this book the words just, justice, unjust, injustice, injustices and "unjustice" are randomly and crookedly placed on the page.

There is a reason for this: you never know which one you are going to get! The court decisions are all over the place and you may as well have bought a lottery ticket.

Justice and injustices are drawn from the lottery pool at random - if you are not one of the affluent or well educated.

If you are wealthy or well educated, or, if you are a relative or friend of the judge, you most likely will get justice.

On the back cover you will notice that the Supreme Court building is upside down and crooked.

There is a reason for this, too: "unjustice" has gotten to the point that justice is totally upside down in this country.

The Supreme Court Justices are put in office by the President - not by the people! And, they are not put there because of their firm commitment to the Constitution!

They're put there because of their stand on specific issues such as gun control, birth control, mining or environmental laws and other popular issues at the time. Perhaps political?

You have to ask yourself a question: is Justice, Injustices, Unjustice upside down in your country?

If you look at the front cover again you will see that the words just and justice are there. But, you've got to look for it - it's hard to find!

It may actually be upside-down because of inadvertence or accident but it is fixable!

After you read this book I'm certain you will want to write your congressman or congresswoman and insist on a congressional hearing about "unjustice"!

It could happen to you!

Be certain to go to www.theunjusticesystem.com website for:

New information;
Other cases;
How to find laws & Rules of Court;
More research information;
And more

Available at all major book retailers:
Ask for "Unjustice" or books by the author "Mac Turney" and at Lulu Books: www.lulu.com

And search for the name: Unjustice,
The Unjustice System or Mac Turney

Unjustice
Published by:
Mac Turney
P. O. Box 537
Stanfield, Arizona 85272-0537

www.ingramcontent.com/pod-product-compliance
Lightning Source LLC
Chambersburg PA
CBHW030819310726
48980CB00006B/554/J
9780578018690